The Pinfire Lady Strikes Back

English aristocrat Abbie Penraven has forged a new life for herself in the West. She has had to fight hard to gain respect and has become known as the Pinfire Lady due to her skill with her pinfire revolver. When Abbie's ranch is raided and her friends kidnapped, she once more takes to the trail, to rescue the stolen ones and destroy the nest of bandits.

By the same author

The Pinfire Lady

The Pinfire Lady Strikes Back

P.J. Gallagher

A Black Horse Western

ROBERT HALE

© P.J. Gallagher 2019
First published in Great Britain 2019

ISBN 978-0-7198-2999-4

The Crowood Press
The Stable Block
Crowood Lane
Ramsbury
Marlborough
Wiltshire SN8 2HR

www.bhwesterns.com

Robert Hale is an imprint
of The Crowood Press

Typeset by
Derek Doyle & Associates, Shaw Heath
Printed and bound in Great Britain by
4Bind Ltd, Stevenage, SG1 2XT

Dedicated to my Mother and Father, long deceased
but always in our thoughts

CHAPTER ONE

Abbie Penraven groaned as she slowly regained consciousness. Though her eyes were still tightly closed, she became aware of a glaring white light overhead whose burning orb was apparent even through her closed lids. Cautiously, she opened her eyes slightly and attempted to see around her.

When she tried to change position, Abbie immediately discovered that her movements were more than restricted; she was completely immobilized and, furthermore, she was stripped naked. Narrowing her eyes and slowly raising her head while ignoring a persistent throbbing at the back of her skull, Abbie stared down towards her feet and then peered to either side.

Her ankles had been lashed with rawhide strips to wooden stakes driven firmly into the hard-packed sandy soil. Her left arm, stretched out at a right angle to her body, was likewise secured to another stake. Abbie turned her head to the right and was surprised to discover that her right wrist was free of any restraint. It was, however, a cruel jest since her right arm was

7

firmly secured to the ground by two stakes either side of her elbow. She could raise her right arm to a vertical position but no further. That limb was tied in such a way that she could bring it no further to either shield her eyes from the burning sun nor indeed engage in any other function such as brushing away any of the persistent flies drawn to the scene by her perspiring body.

Neatly piled, carefully out of reach on her right side, was her buckskin clothing, boots, hat and gun-belt, which still contained her holstered pinfire revolver, alongside was her Bowie knife, driven into the ground, and looped around the haft was her military canteen which she recalled filling at a small mountain spring earlier.

Abbie stretched out, straining with all of her might to try and reach either knife or water bottle. It was an impossible venture. Whoever had placed her in this position knew exactly what he was doing. Food and water were just out of reach. A sharp blade capable of cutting her bonds was impossible to get to. These objects were deliberately placed to tease her while the burning sun would drive her mad with both thirst and the pain of acute sunburn.

Abbie attempted to recall the events that had ended with her in such a perilous situation.

She had spent an afternoon paying a long overdue visit to the elderly English ladies who ran the haberdashery store in Colorado City. After several cups of tea, she had finally managed to take her leave and started heading back to the ranch at a leisurely pace. From the city to the horse ranch was approximately 7 miles and Abbie had accomplished but 2 miles of her journey when she noted a wisp of smoke rising above the trees ahead of her.

Her first thought was totally irrelevant as she remembered Jack Harding's comment when his wife, Dora, had burnt some of her hitherto delicious hot biscuits, 'Ullo, I see that Dora's done a King Alfred trick on us!' And Abbie smiled at her recollection. This smoke, however, was no smiling matter as it rose in a thick column into the still air. Either the ranch house or the outbuildings were on fire, and now she could hear the distant sound of gunshots so Abbie urged her bay gelding into a gallop.

The remaining miles seemed to take forever to cover and all the while Abbie was wondering who had decided to attack her ranch. Comanche? There had been no report of hostile Indians being in the area for some time. In fact, a small band of Utes were camped in one of the home paddocks engaged in breaking some of her half-wild stock. Renegades of the calibre of Scar and his gang of cutthroats that she and her wagon train had eliminated while travelling west? Abbie put all conjectures out of her mind and concentrated on getting home as swiftly as the bay's hoofs would cover the distance.

Drawing closer, she could hear yells of rage amid screams of fear from burning tepees in the west paddock and roars of exultant triumph coming from raiders now vanishing among the trees. The barns, bunkhouse and the ranch house were on fire with flames leaping from the broken windows and already licking their way across the cedar shakes of the roofs.

A male figure lay face down on the ground in front of the porch and Abbie, throwing herself from the saddle, dropped down beside him with an anguished cry of, 'Jack! Jack Harding! Answer me! What's happened?' as she had frantically tried to roll her foreman over onto his back, dreading the while at what she might yet discover.

Abbie succeeded in her attempts and was horrified to see Jack's face covered with blood. Dipping her bandanna in the nearby water trough, she wiped his face carefully and was relieved to discover that the blood was coming from a long furrow on the right side of his head where he had been creased by a bullet. Jack groaned, opened his eyes and said, 'They've got Dora.' Then he lapsed back into unconsciousness.

As Abbie looked around wildly for assistance, other survivors of the raid emerged from where they had hidden. Among them was Joey, who crawled out from under the porch with an empty pistol clutched in his right hand. He told Abbie a tale of how word had arrived at the ranch that rustlers were making off with a large herd of horses some distance away and how Jack had sent most of their riders in pursuit accompanied by some of the Ute braves.

The raiders had struck less than an hour later, riding in from the south whooping, yelling and shooting down any resistance. Jack, Joey and some of the remaining hands put up a spirited defence but were swamped by the sheer numbers of their attackers and they were quickly overcome. The ranch was looted and then the buildings set on fire. Joey confirmed Jack's statement as he had seen Dora kicking and screaming in the hands of the men who carried her off.

Abbie quickly made up her mind. 'Joey! I want you to find a horse, ride to town and bring back Doctor Stevens. Make it fast. We must have other wounded people here or over in the Ute camp.'

Joey scuttled off and shortly thereafter could be seen riding at a gallop down the trail to Colorado City. His mount, a small Shetland pony, had been considered not worthwhile stealing by the raiders, who had cleaned out the horse corrals of the ranch.

Other hands, including Wu Hang, the Chinese cook, helped Abbie get Jack to a small shelter that had escaped the fires. Fortunately the half-buried storehouse remained intact and from its cool interior Abbie was able to forage and obtain supplies with which to fill her saddle-bags. Her intention was very plain. Abbie was filled with a cold steely resolution to get out immediately after these miscreants who had dared to attack her property and her friends.

Abbie gave Wu Hang careful explicit instructions to take care of Mr Jack until the doctor arrived: save all that could be salvaged from the burning buildings and inform the riders, who would be coming in after their futile pursuit of the fictional rustlers, to await instructions from Mr Jack. Abbie did not want an angry bunch of riders behind her who would be likely to fire at anything that was moving and which would probably mean that she would be between two fires.

Mounting her bay, she rode over to the Ute camp, noting the still figures lying on the ground and the few dazed survivors, mostly elderly people who were attempting to save some of their limited belongings.

Abbie expressed her sympathy to the bewildered old folk, promising them that their dead relations would not go unavenged. Then, spurring the bay into a canter, she commenced to trail the marauders as she entered the forested area south of the ranch.

Abbie preceded with care, moving slowly and observing traces of the passage of many horses, some carrying riders. There were hoof-prints in the mulch-laden flooring of the forest, frequent horse droppings and very occasionally shreds of cloth caught at rider-height amid the branches either side of the trail. Periodically, Abbie halted and listened, interpreting the many natural sounds of the bush.

Finally, her patience was rewarded. During one stop she distinctly heard a cry of pain. The voice was that of a female and Abbie wondered if she had been lucky enough to come upon Dora this early in her search. Tying the bay securely to a convenient branch, she crept silently through the undergrowth in the direction from which she was sure the sound had come. She was rewarded by the noise of yet another cry, one of pain mingled with a strangled sob that was cut off in mid-voice by the sound of a slap and a gruff command, 'Shut up or it'll be worse for yu!'

Abbie peered cautiously through the bushes into a little clearing just in time to see one bearded brute end

12

his rape of the young Ute girl Yellow Flower, whom she recalled coming to the ranch house. The rapist rose to his feet and nodded to his swarthy companion, 'Now, *amigo*. It's your turn. Make it snappy. The gang will be getting too far ahead of us!'

His partner nodded, grinned and undid his fly buttons as Abbie pushed through the bushes pistol in hand and grimly ordered the unsavoury couple to get their hands in the air. Both men turned in the direction of the voice and simultaneously, rather than obeying the command, they both grabbed for their holstered handguns. Filled with rage at the evil pair, Abbie did not hesitate but shot both of them in the head and also in the crotch for good measure, although in truth her second shots were wasted since for both men the bullets in the head had already ended their earthly existence.

The Ute girl sat on the ground, her head buried in her arms and, rocking back and forth, she wept in anguish. Abbie reloaded her pistol and sat beside the victim, holding her and stroking her hair as she attempted to give her words of comfort. After a while Yellow Flower raised her head and, taking Abbie's right hand, she pressed it to her lips in gratitude and with signs indicated she would never forget her rescuer.

Abbie nodded and smiled, wishing the while that she had listened more carefully when Billy Curtis had attempted to teach her common Indian words. Finally, she rose and pulled the girl to her feet. Pointing to her and then to the two horses belonging to the dead outlaws, Abbie indicated she should take them and

13

ride back to the ranch to inform somebody that she, Abbie, was still trailing the raiders.

Puzzled, Yellow Flower frowned and then, apparently understanding Abbie's instructions, nodded. She bent down and relieved one of the corpses of gun-belt and pistol and also acquired a murderous-looking Arkansas Toothpick with a blade at least 10in long. Then, giving Abbie a warm hug, she crossed to the patiently waiting horses. Riding one and leading the other, with a wave of farewell she headed north as Abbie returned to the place where she had left her bay gelding.

The raiders' trail continued to lead due south, and Abbie tracked them with no difficulty but with great care, pausing whenever she topped a rise in the ever-changing terrain. Gradually the wooded slopes gave way to more open country with the low hills broken up into numerous gullies and arroyos, any of which could conceal the enemies she was pursuing.

On the evening of the fourth day, as the western sun sank towards the horizon, Abbie halted her bay and slowly and carefully scrutinized her surroundings. For some time she had been travelling through a landscape that was becoming more and more parched as the grass gave way to red sandy soil, and the lack of water suggested that she was approaching a desert area. In fact, she was on the edge of the area known to the Spanish explorers as the *Llano Estacado*, the Staked Plain.

Narrowing her eyes against the sun, Abbie noticed a very thin column of smoke rising from beyond a rise in

14

the ground to her left. Turning off the trail, she had found a place of concealment where she could tether her horse in a clump of mesquite bushes, close, yet hidden from the trail. Then, as twilight descended, she had crept silently towards the location of the smoke, realizing full well that whoever had lit a fire could be Indian, hostile or otherwise, an innocent traveller or, hopefully, a member of the gang she was chasing.

Drawing closer to her objective, she could distinctly hear the sound of male voices, and she dropped to her stomach and crawled carefully to the top of the rise. Raising her head slowly, she surveyed the scene below in the arroyo. There were four or five men seated smoking and drinking around a small fire, on the far side of which lay a bound and gagged figure wearing a dimly perceived print dress that Abbie was sure that she had seen Dora wearing around the ranch. As Abbie lifted her head slightly to get a better view, she was suddenly aware of a shape looming up beside her. Something crashed down on her head and she lost consciousness.

The heavy crunching of footsteps brought Abbie back from her review of the events that had led her to her present perilous situation. She opened her eyes and. narrowing them against the glare of the afternoon sun. she sought to determine the owner of the approaching steps. With her limited vision, she could see nobody and decided that the visitor was behind her. Listening carefully, she noted that the footsteps were uneven, as though the owner was having some difficulty mounting the slope to where Abbie was staked out.

The sound of footsteps ceased and moments later a harsh voice chuckled, saying, 'Well, I must say! You've got yourself in a pretty pickle! Don't you feel it's a little warm lying out in the sun like that?'

The jeering voice sounded familiar and as he moved around to the east, thus still allowing the hot sun to play on Abbie's already burning flesh, she recognized her captor and tormentor. It was Bart Bradshaw, the late Roger Fenton's foreman, with whom she had had a duel the first day she had gone into Colorado City. Abbie tried to keep her tone casual, believing that it would not help her if she showed fear to such as him. 'Good afternoon, Mr Bradshaw! Out for a little stroll?' and then, making a verbal jab, 'I see that you have acquired quite a limp, sir. Did you perhaps have a little accident?'

Bradshaw cursed her with many a foul oath, stating that she had taken advantage of him when they first met and he had sworn to have his revenge. 'At first I hoped that Fenton would have beaten you, but he turned out to be just a broken reed, and I had to find a place to lay up 'til my wounds healed. That leg wound will never get better, so the doctors say, an' I've got you to blame for me being a cripple.'

Totally ignoring the fact that he had drawn his pistol on Abbie first during their encounter, Bradshaw continued with his tirade, his voice getting louder with every word and spittle forming at the corners of his mouth, 'Now I've got you where I want you an' you're gonner die a long slow painful death. You'll finally be praying for death to take you. By that time the sun will have either turned you into a babbling idiot or you will be burnt so badly that your skin will flake off in sheets. I wish that I could be here to see it but I've got business elsewhere. I guess you'd like a small drink before I go!' he picked up Abbie's canteen and callously poured a small quantity on the ground just out of reach, before replacing the container in its original position.

'There! That's to remind you of what water looks like! It's the last you'll see, Miss Pinfire!' And with this parting remark Bart Bradshaw turned away and limped down the slope.

Abbie shivered. Although she had maintained a brave face while Bradshaw had been present, inwardly she had begun to quake at the horrible fate that he had in store for her. There was yet another possible death that he had omitted to mention and that was the chance of being located by some wandering predator and being eaten alive. She began to panic and tore wildly at the rawhide strips restraining her but only succeeded in ripping the flesh from her ankles and left wrist. She desisted and lay there panting with her exertions and fighting a desire to despair and surrender to her miserable destiny.

CHAPTER TWO

Night fell, but with a full moon and a blanket of twinkling stars against a black velvet background, it wasn't really dark. Initially, Abbie relished the cool touch of the evening breeze after the fiery heat of the day but after a short while her body gave an involuntary shiver and she realized that as it grew colder through the night, ironically she would be longing for the warmth of the sun.

Suddenly she was aware of movement close by and, straining her eyes, tried to determine what it was that was creeping closer and closer. A wolf? A mountain lion? She did not relish being the main course for some carnivore and was about to yell and scream in attempt to startle the intruder when a small hand covered her mouth and a voice whispered, 'Shh!' Abbie lay still as swiftly a sharp object cut through the bonds securing her and then she was helped slowly to her feet. Her rescuer gathered up Abbie's belongings and, taking her by the hand, led her gently down the hill and away to where her bay along with the two other horses waited patiently.

It was then that Abbie realized just who had delivered her from the awful fate that Bart Bradshaw had in store for her and she clutched Yellow Flower in gratitude, trying meanwhile to avoid breaking into tears. The Indian girl patted her gently, murmuring some words of sympathy, and then, urging Abbie to mount her bay, she led the way into the tangle of hills, deliberately going over rocky places that would leave no trace of their passing. Finally, she halted and helped Abbie down. Reaction had set in and she shivered while at the same time her sun-burnt skin felt it was on fire. Abbie was so stiff that she moved like an old woman and when Yellow Flower offered her the canteen she would have drank the whole contents if not restrained.

Abbie was preparing to try and don her clothing when Yellow Flower signalled her to wait. The Ute girl vanished into the night and returned shortly bearing handfuls of leaves, which she crushed and mixed with a small quantity of animal fat obtained from a pouch. Then she proceeded to gently rub the creamy mixture all over Abbie's face and body. The white girl noted that the salve had an immediate soothing effect and in a very short time the burning sensation had ceased.

The application of Yellow Flower's ointment enabled Abbie to literally slither into her clothing and, after doing so, the two girls curled up and attempted to get some much-needed sleep. Abbie was so tired that she ignored her normal bedtime precautions but she was quite safe in the location chosen by the Ute girl and they had an undisturbed night.

In the morning they broke their fast by sharing a can of baked beans, some dried-out biscuits and water from their canteens. Then Abbie insisted that she check their firearms, not only her 12mm pinfire but also the .36 Navy Colt that Yellow Flower had taken from one of the dead rapists. Abbie unloaded the latter pistol and showed the Ute girl how to load it with powder, wad and ball and how to cap the nipples. Yellow Flower watched Abbie intently and nodded to show that she understood the procedure.

Abbie would have liked to question her as to why she had not gone back to the ranch but found it too difficult since they did not have a language each understood. She could only assume that they had a mutual bond since in turn they had both rescued each other. Abbie next decided that they had to develop some common terms, starting with their names. She pointed at herself and said, 'Abbie! Me, Abbie!' Pointing at the girl, she raised her eyes to make a soundless question. Yellow Flower caught on and gave a long Ute reply, and Abbie realized that she would have to rename her Indian friend. She frowned in thought and then smiled.

Having read Mr Longfellow's account of 'Hiawatha' shortly after it was published, Abbie decided that she had the perfect name. Mini-Ha-Ha was far too long so, pointing at herself once more, she again said, 'Abbie,' then pointing to Yellow Flower she said, 'Minny' and again 'Minny'. Frowning a little, the Ute repeated the name and in this fashion Abbie acquired a friend and companion named Minny.

Glancing through the trees at the position of the sun, Abbie decided that it was still early mid-morning and it was time that she and her companion planned the next part of their tasks to free Dora and get back at least some of the stolen horses. Thinking back to Bradshaw's jeering comments, Abbie came to the conclusion that he intended to return to view and get satisfaction from seeing the effect on her of being exposed to the searing heat of the desert sun for a full day. His previous visit had been in late afternoon, as best she could estimate, therefore she and Minny had several hours in which to launch a rescue operation.

Smoothing out an area of sand, she drew a sketch map drawing triangles and using stones to represent the Ute camp and the ranch. Then she marked a long line to indicate the trail south. Two stick figures were the two rapists and a line through them and pointing to Minny showed their fate. In a similar way Abbie showed herself as staked out and rescued and close by a valley with Dora bound and gagged. This last part she explained using mime to imitate Dora's predicament. Finally, Abbie tried to determine the number of enemies immediately opposing them. A series of stick figures represented Bradshaw, and being on the safe side, five figures to represent the men in the valley and a sixth one, the person who had bashed her on the head and rendered her unconscious. Abbie had long since come to the conclusion the scene she had seen in the little valley had been posed, which in turn suggested that she had been under observation for some time before her capture.

She decided that to launch a rescue it would be important to make a wide detour and get ahead of where Bradshaw and his men were camped in the little valley. This she imparted to Minny via her sand map and suggested that the Indian girl plan the route to bring them out ahead of the gang. There was one other thing puzzling Abbie. Where were all the other raiders and the horses that had been stolen? These problems, however, she put out of her mind for the time being in order to concentrate on the immediate task at hand.

Minny knew exactly what was expected of her and, moving cautiously but confidently, took them both on dim trails that kept them well to the west of the main north–south route. Finally, in the early afternoon Minny called a halt and, pointing north with her left hand, whispered one word, 'Badsaw', which Abbie took to be the Ute rendition of Bradshaw.

CHAPTER THREE

Their three horses were tethered in a small grove of trees, and with Minny leading they crept silently through the bushes until they were on the brush-covered edge of the small valley. Peering very cautiously, Abbie observed the scene below her. Six men were lounging around the fire; four were playing a listless game of cards while Bradshaw and one other were laying on their backs dozing – the remaining figure, that of Dora, sat without a gag but bound hand and foot against a sandy bank. Abbie and Minny waited patiently.

Finally they were rewarded by the appearance of yet a seventh outlaw who rode in from the north and dis-mounted by the group. The two watchers distinctly heard him render his report to Bradshaw, 'Well, Boss! There's nary a sign of anyone amoving down the trail from Harding's ranch. So I guess that pinfire she-cat was the only one who got quickly on our trail. I didn't go up the hill ter check on her but there was no noise so maybe she's croaked!'

One of the card players interjected in a challenging voice. 'So let's get this little personal vendetta over with! *El Caudillo* is gonner be wondering what the hell has happened to us. An' I for one don't intend to cross that one!'

'Goddamit, Wolf! Jus' shut your goddam mouth or I'm likely to shut it for you. I told the Chief that I had a little personal score to settle when we planned this raid an' he knew we'd be a little late getting to La Cruz. We'll soon get there an' can turn over this piece of merchandise,' pointing to Dora, 'get our money for it and the horses an' all relax in the cantinas.

'Now who's coming with me ter check on my piece of fried meat? She should be a lovely sight by now!' None of the men volunteered and so Bradshaw called out one name: 'Felipe! You're the youngest and there-fore probably the most agile. You can help me up the hill. Agreed?'

Felipe muttered an almost inaudible '*Sí, señor!*' and reluctantly got to his feet. With Bradshaw, he crossed to where the horses were tethered and, selecting two, they mounted and rode north to the hill where sup-posedly Abbie was still staked out.

Abbie motioned to Minny and they worked their way along the rim to where it was decided that Dora would not be in danger from crossfire, and then both slipped and wriggled down the sandy sides to stand upright in the little valley. Hearing noise during their last several feet of movement the outlaws looked up, momentarily frozen by the girls' sudden appearance in their hide-out. Then they sprang to their feet, drawing their pistols and cursing at being surprised. Abbie and Minny had already drawn their guns and Abbie in particular was firing and hitting with her usual deadly accuracy while Minny also fired, though in truth, her shots were going wild but had the effect of causing the outlaws to distribute their return fire.

Two of Abbie's selected targets were already down and still and a third stood empty-handed clutching his stomach before sinking to his knees. Minny had fired four shots and one by chance had hit one of the gang in the shoulder, prompting him to drop his pistol. The fifth member of the unsavoury bunch was unhurt and, as Abbie swiftly reloaded, he scrabbled around seeking his pistol, a cumbersome pepperbox. Not having time to complete her reloading, Abbie drew her Bowie knife and threw it underhand as Billy Curtis had taught her. The 10in blade skimmed through the air and sliced into the outlaw's solar plexus. He gave a surprised grunt and collapsed, clasping her knife as though determined to retain his new possession.

Grey gun-smoke twirled up from the valley as Abbie, having completed her reloading, ran forward, retrieving her Bowie from the dying outlaw. Then, crossing to where Dora lay, she quickly severed her bonds.

The two rescuers helped Dora to her feet, where she stood swaying for a moment as she attempted to get the blood coursing through her veins. Turning to Abbie with tears rolling down her cheeks and her bottom lip trembling, she said, 'I knew you wouldn't forget me, Captain!' Then with a touch of her old wry humour, 'What took you so long?' And she threw herself into Abbie's arms while at the same time drawing Minny to her so that the trio stood for a moment locked in a tight embrace.

Suddenly the emotion of their reunion was shattered by a familiar harsh voice. 'How touching! Now I've got you all together in one group! Move aside, you two.' Looking up. they saw Bart Bradshaw with his pistol drawn in his right hand while with his left he gesticulated to emphasize his command that Dora and Minny move away from Abbie. Reluctantly. the two latter girls did as they were ordered. leaving Abbie standing by herself facing Bradshaw flanked by Felipe, the young Mexican outlaw.

'Now, you hellcat, I've finally got you where there's no escape. Sure you can go for that pistol if you've got a mind to do so but at the slightest move you're going to get it. Felipe! Keep those other women covered!'

CHAPTER FOUR

Felipe raised the double-barreled 10-gauge shotgun that he carried but, rather than obeying Bradshaw's command, he swung it suddenly to cover his late leader. 'No señor! I think that it is you who must drop his gun. I stand with these ladies!'

Bradshaw cursed and started to turn towards his erstwhile follower, and Felipe pulled both triggers of his shotgun. Almost cut in two by the volume of buckshot, the outlaw's body was thrown several feet by the violence of the impact. Turning towards Dora, Felipe said, 'Señora Harding. Did I not promise you that no harm would come to either you or your friends? See. I have kept my promise!'

Abbie looked enquiringly at Dora, who nodded, 'Felipe is right, Abbie. He was the only one who tried to comfort me while I was held captive. He would whisper encouragement and loosen my bonds whenever he could and brought me water while the others were content to see me go thirsty. Felipe is OK!'

Abbie turned back to Felipe and suggested that he

27

explain why he had joined the raiding party that had attacked the ranch. Felipe described how his sister Juanita had been chosen by *El Caudillo* to be his 'favourite' woman, that is his mistress, until he would become tired of her and hand her over to his men. The Mexican boy thought that it would go badly with his sister if he did not volunteer. '*El Caudillo* he is one very evil man, *señorita*. Everybody fear him and his anger!'

Attention was then given to the one other remaining member of the outlaw band who still stood holding his shoulder, which had been shattered by Minny's bullet. Both Dora and Abbie were prepared reluctantly to tend the unsavoury captive's wound but Minny shook her head violently as she burst forth with a stream of voluble Ute pointing to the outlaw's belt. The others looked to where she was pointing and saw the black-haired scalp hanging from his belt still showing signs of fresh blood, which indicated that it must have been taken recently.

Minny spoke excitedly in her own language and from the gestures it was evident that she was demanding the death of the wounded outlaw. In response to her outburst, both Abbie and Dora were shaking their heads, being reluctant to be considered cold-blooded executioners. Meanwhile, the outlaw taking advantage of the fact that their attention was not on him, had been edging further away from the group towards the saddled horses. Suddenly he made a dash for freedom.

Felipe reacted fastest. Pulling a large knife from his belt, he hurled it as the fleeing man attempted to

28

mount a dirty grey gelding. The Mexican lad's aim was true and his knife buried itself to the haft between the outlaw's shoulder blades. He clung to the saddle for a moment and then his fingers loosed their grip and he slumped down and lay in a huddled heap between the legs of the horse.

'Felipe!' cried an outraged Abbie. 'You didn't have to kill the man. He was our prisoner and couldn't get very far!'

Felipe explained why he had reacted so quickly. If his fellow countryman, whom he called Juan, had succeeded in escaping he would have headed straight for La Cruz and *El Caudillo* would have mounted an immediate expedition to avenge the deaths of Bradshaw and his men. Furthermore, and in Felipe's mind, of far more importance, the bandit chieftain would have undoubtedly exacted some terrible punishment upon Juanita, the boy's sister.

Mollified by the Mexican's explanation, Abbie said no more about the matter and also ignored the sight of Minny doing some kind of victory dance around the corpse. 'All right, people! Let's strip these bodies of any worthwhile guns and ammunition and get away from this valley; there are just too many dead around here to make it a jolly campsite.'

The four of them worked quickly, removing gun-belts and powder flasks and placing them together with the firearms in a pile. They found that they had a mixed hoard of flintlock and percussion-lock long guns and handguns. Three Colts and a British Adams were the only handguns worth keeping and two of the relatively late model rifles. The remainder were thrown into the undergrowth and then the four, now well-armed and having retrieved their patient horses, moved to a different camp site chosen by Minny. Abbie decided to hold a council of war to determine their next step.

Her decision, however, had to be deferred as Minny placed an ear on the ground and indicated by sign language that many horses were on the trail. Before the quartet had time to react, she listened again and pointed to the north, suggesting that the newcomers were coming south from the far-off ranch.

Abbie had them move to a defensive position overlooking the trail and there they waited until the oncoming strangers hove in sight. At last a compact body of riders appeared, headed by none other than Jack Harding, hatless, but with a white bandage almost like a turban swathing his head.

Abbie fired three shots in quick succession, the universally acknowledged signal of recognition, and the column of riders brought their mounts to a halt in a flurry of dust. 'Hallo, Jack!' she cried, waving her arms in the air, and her actions were copied by Dora and her companions.

Dora ran forward and threw herself into Jack's arms, smothering him with kisses. Abbie followed more casually, appraising the host of riders accompanying her foreman. Minny was quickly surrounded by a group of young Ute braves who eyed her up and down, noting enviously the weaponry she was carrying, and Felipe hung back, not too sure how all these people would

30

react to his presence.

It was quickly decided by the two leaders, Abbie and Jack, to establish camp and, after posting guards and cooking a hasty meal, to have a discussion as to the next step that should be taken by the column.

They all gathered in a circle around a smouldering campfire. Abbie, seated next to Jack and Dora, looked around her at the assembled people, more than a little surprised by the number and who was there.

Going clockwise on Jack's left there were eight men from the ranch and it was two of their number who were on guard. Beyond them were six volunteers from Abbie's gold mine and beyond them a medley of people who had come to assist their former wagon captain. They included the Smiths, Bobby and his mother; Anne Marlowe, accompanied by a tough bearded stranger introduced as 'my man'; and Jacob Levy. Minny's contingent consisted of herself and seven capable-looking young braves, a couple of whom had already salvaged two of the discarded long guns that had been thrown away from the valley of the dead outlaws.

Continuing around the circle, there were three townspeople from Colorado City, with whom she only had a nodding acquaintanceship, and to complete the assembly before her, Wilf Bateson and his team of five gunners, together with their two-pounder mountain gun. Jack had already explained to Abbie that Bateson had contacted him when the column was being organized and offered his services together with his artillery piece. Jack had welcomed the addition since,

31

as he said, 'You never know when a bit of heavier fire-power will come in useful!'

There was one other. Felipe sat close to Abbie as inconspicuously as possible, still uncertain of how he was being received and frequently casting a wary eye upon the Ute braves. Altogether there were now, including herself, just shy of forty people available for further action.

Abbie opened the proceedings by describing lucidly what had happened since she had left the ranch. She did not dwell upon Minny's horrible experience, neither did she call it rape since she did not know how revealing that crime would affect the girl's future. Minny had merely been attacked and she had been lucky enough to rescue her before much harm was done. Likewise, she glossed over her own experience, stressing only that Minny had rescued her. With regard to Felipe, she described in great detail how he had been forced to ride with the outlaws and had him wriggling with embarrassment as she detailed how he finished the career of Bart Bradshaw.

Jack then told quickly how, with Doctor Steven's care, he had made a swift recovery and immediately started organizing a punitive expedition. He pointed out that many other people had wanted to come along but he thought that it would be best to avoid an unwieldy number, which could easily become a mob. Abbie had noticed several pack horses and upon being asked about them Jack described how Benson the general store owner had been most generous, furnishing stocks of dried and canned food along with powder caps and shot. Abbie smiled. Benson knew which side his bread was buttered on – especially since she owned his store!

'Now,' she said. 'We have recapped events to date. We've rescued Dora and Minny, I mean Yellow Flower, and we have wiped out Bradshaw's gang of cutthroats. The horses are still missing but I can handle their loss with no problem. What do you folks think should be the next step? Go on or return home?' Abbie deliberately put the question this way as she did not want to be the one deciding to put people's lives in danger.

She continued, 'Before we hear from any of you, I think that you should hear from Felipe since he lived among the outlaws and knows what we are up against. Felipe.' Abbie motioned the Mexican to his feet.

Felipe stood grasping his straw sombrero in both hands and moving it round and round. He was speechless until Abbie put her left arm around his thin shoulders and gave him a squeeze. He smiled and nodded.

'Well, *señores* and *señoras*, maybe I can tell you first about La Cruz. It was a mission built by the good Franciscan Fathers about one hundred and twenty years ago. They had hoped to convert the wild Comanche and for a little while they were successful. But then the Comanche attacked the mission and killed the priests, brothers and many people that they had converted. The ruined church and the buildings were, how do you say, destroyed – but not altogether.

'Other people came and thought that this was a good place to hide out if they were running from the law. My father, he was what we call a political. He was against the government and the Rurales would like to catch him, so we left Mexico and came north to La Cruz; my father, my mother, my baby sister Juanita and myself. The village was not so bad then. We had a good well. Pablo Morales kept a little store and it was also a cantina.

'My father built a little hut. We grew some beans and had chickens and one little pig We were a happy family for some years and my father, he thought that one day we would all go back to Mexico if there was a new El Presidente. Then one evil day came seniors, *El Caudillo* arrived in La Cruz with his comancheros. He said that he was the boss, the chief, and everyone must obey him in every regard. If his men wanted something they just took it and soon our chickens and the family pet, our pig, had been stolen from us. My father, he protested, and the thieves laughed and just said speak to *El Caudillo*. My father was a brave man and did so, and that spawn of the devil had him tied to a post in front of the ruined church and then his men used him for target practice.

'My father's murder, for that is what it was, killed my mother, but she died slowly, worn out trying to earn a few coppers to feed my sister and me. After my mother had died, we two were looked after by our neighbours the way poor people will help each other until the terrible day when *El Caudillo* was walking around the village and saw Juanita before we could hide her. He declared that she was to be his wife but, of course, he lied. There was no ceremony, he took her to be his woman until he gets tired of her, and then she will be handed over to his men.

'*El Caudillo* has maybe forty to fifty *pistoleros*. Some Mexican, some *gringos*, some half-breeds and some renegade Indians. Most of them are well-armed but I don't know how well they will fight. One more thing *senores*, if you decide to attack I can draw a very good map of La Cruz on the ground. Thank you for listening to me.' And Felipe sat down amid a round of applause from his listeners.

Speaker after speaker rose to express the view that the expedition should continue with the avowed aim of smashing *El Caudillo* and his evil regime, while at the same time doing everything possible to avoid innocent bloodshed. One person emphasized a generally held opinion that unless the renegades were destroyed nobody would be safe since they could always raid north from La Cruz.

One of the Utes expressed the Indian point of view more bluntly. Their lodges had been attacked and certain of their people killed. The victims' spirits would not rest until they were avenged. Even if the White Eyes chose to return northward, the Ute would gather more of their people and plan an attack against *El Caudillo*.

Wilf Bateson stood up and stressed that he and his gun team hadn't hauled 'ole Betsy', their mountain artillery piece, all this way just as an exercise. They wanted to hear the cannon roar in anger, which remark caused a ripple of laughter to go around the assembled circle.

Having heard all the comments, Abbie rose and addressed the group. 'Very well! Since we seem to be agreed that we must wipe out this nest of vipers I suggest we consider a number of points. First, we will be attacking determined men who may be well fortified and to be of an equal number we need more volunteers. Jack, can you get more from both the ranch and the mine?' Jack replied that he would send a messenger and would double his men within two or three days.

White Cloud, speaking for the Utes, indicated that if messengers were sent he could triple the Indian contingent and one of their number started off there and then to summon more braves to the war party.

By unanimous consent, Abbie was appointed leader of the expedition. It was a strange decision considering the time and the place but she had proved herself extremely capable when leading a wagon train. She had demonstrated that she kept a very cool head, whether commanding a defensive situation or facing down a solitary gunman. Because of her upbringing in India in a military establishment, she almost automatically had an air of command.

In a few days the numbers in the punitive column had more than doubled as more Indians and whites made their appearance. Abbie and Jack, her second in command, were anxious to move since the numbers were likely to exhaust the available food supplies in a very short time.

Finally, with scouting parties of Indians ranging ahead, the column moved out. Jack, realizing that some kind of military order was essential, had divided the men into groups of between fifteen to twenty, each one under the command of a competent squad leader. Jacob Levy was added to what Jack called the Head Quarters staff. Jacob was in charge of food and ammunition, and five volunteers were attached to the gun team to give them additional rifle fire if required.

Abbie, riding at the head of the column, thought about her unique situation. 'My father would, I believe, be very proud that I've stepped, as it were, almost automatically into a position of military authority. I now have an added responsibility. I must try to make sure that I do not conduct myself in any way of which he would not approve.'

CHAPTER FIVE

The terrain through which the column was passing was changing with every mile, and the trees became sparse and the hilly country changed to an increasingly arid plain. At the end of that first day they made a waterless camp and the men were warned to have but small smokeless fires with which to make coffee. Night fell and with it the temperature as the dry air of the desert failed to retain the warmth of the day. The night was cold and Abbie realized that too many days of this contrast – blistering heat by day, freezing cold by night – would eat rapidly away at the morale.

Therefore she suggested to Jack that they do a night march to bring them closer to La Cruz and hopefully reduce the duration of acute discomfort. Jack agreed and about midnight the weary men saddled their horses and continued south by the light of a million glittering stars and a bright yellow moon.

One of their Ute scouts returned with the news that so far they had not detected any outposts north of La Cruz, which would seem to indicate that so far *El*

Caudillo had not realized that Bart Bradshaw and his men were not returning and therefore they did not need to increase their defences. The scout drew a sketch map on the ground to show that just north of the mission was a deep arroyo running from east to west and bisecting the north–south trail. The Indians thought that if the column made another night march they could take shelter in the arroyo and thus be hidden from any prying eyes but be ready to make a dawn attack.

Abbie and Jack consulted with Felipe, who reckoned that by morning they would be perhaps a day's ride from La Cruz. It was therefore decided to rest up during the day, enduring the blistering heat as well as they could and then make yet another night march as suggested.

Felipe turned to Abbie, 'Señorita Abbie! Would you permit me to offer a suggestion?'

She nodded to him. 'Go ahead Felipe! What do you have in mind?'

'Well it is like this. I have been thinking about the villagers, the poor honest people stuck in La Cruz when we attack. They are innocent but they will be, how do you say, between the devil and the deep blue sea. I should like to go ahead with maybe three or four men and bring them out into the desert west of the village and then into the arroyo where they will be safe during the fighting.'

Abbie looked at Jack, who shrugged his shoulders. 'Well, captain! If he could pull it off it would be a good thing, 'cos then we'd know that those left in the area were the enemy an' we wouldn't be shooting just anyone.'

She turned away to look at Felipe, intently concerned that the Mexican boy's offer was not completely altruistic. 'Tell me truthfully, Felipe! Are you suggesting this so that you can hope to rescue your sister, Juanita?'

Felipe shook his head violently from side to side. 'No, señorita! I swear by all the saints that I did not even consider my poor sister. I know that she will be held close to *El Caudillo* and there is nothing I can do to save her now. Maybe during the attack it will be different.'

Abbie was silent for a few moments as she considered the options. 'Very well, we shall do as Felipe proposes.' She held up her hand to still any possible protest, 'And I will go with the party to reconnoitre the mission so that we will have a better knowledge of what we're up against.'

Reluctantly, Jack agreed, but with the proviso that if the rescue party wasn't back by sun up he would be attacking with the whole force that same day!

CHAPTER SIX

The column reached the arroyo at about two o'clock in the morning and most of the men settled down to try and get some rest with the stern warning, 'Remember! No fires!'

Three men were stationed along the lip of the arroyo as lookouts, staring south towards the tumbled mass of buildings that even at this late hour still showed here and there glimpses of flickering lights, indicating that some people were still abroad. Abbie and Felipe, with three Indians as their escort, prepared to go into La Cruz. Each had equipped himself with the weapons with which he or she was most familiar. Abbie had, of course, her trusty pinfire, her Bowie and for good measure a borrowed .31 calibre Pocket Colt thrust through her belt at her back behind her shirt. Felipe had a pair of pistols as well as the knife with which he had ended the career of one of Bart Bradshaw's men. All three Indians had traded their long guns for bows and arrows and, of course, had their knives as well as tomahawks. With whispered farewells and fervent handshakes, the little party moved out.

Crouching low to reduce their outlined silhouettes against the night sky, they ran swiftly across the desert towards the cluster of huts. Reaching the first one, Felipe motioned them to keep down while he crept around to the blanket-draped doorway. Quietly he raised the covering and vanished into the dark interior. Abbie and the three Utes heard a stifled gasp, followed by a whispered murmuring of voices.

The blanket rose and two adults emerged clutching the hands of three sleepy toddlers and a hastily gathered bundle of their belongings. Felipe pointed out the direction they were to take and with nods of the head they fearfully set off to put distance between themselves and the village. Felipe then moved on to the next hovel and gradually they worked their way through all of the dwellings occupied by the impoverished Mexicans.

Abbie began to think that they would succeed in clearing out all of the villagers without interruption but it was not to be. The occupants of the last hut had just emerged and were being directed to depart northwest in the direction of the arroyo when there was a loud shout and a party of bandits bore down upon them.

'Felipe!' cried Abbie. 'Get these people clear! I and the three braves will cover you. Get moving!'

So saying, Abbie drew her pistol and, taking cover beside the wall of the last hut, opened fire upon the advancing bandits. Simultaneously, the three Utes melted into concealment and moments later their arrows were finding their marks among the yelling outlaws. Abbie fired deliberately and slowly with great effect and every one of her shots found its mark. Her firing and the arrows, which struck down yet more of the foe, caused the attack to wither away from the deadly fire but more of the bandits arrived and spread themselves between the huts. Soon Abbie realized that they were being surrounded.

Their position was rapidly becoming untenable as more and more bandits entered the fray. It was not that they were such great shots but the sheer volume of their fire was causing Abbie to keep her head down, emerging just to take a snap shot and then quickly ducking back under cover.

She called out to her Indian companions, 'Time to get out of here! Let's go!' Only two of the Utes responded. The third was lying on the ground, spread-eagled where he had fallen from the roof of one of the huts and with blood pouring from the result of an unlucky head shot. The other two needed no second command but slipped away into the night.

Abbie had turned to follow their example when she suddenly felt a violent blow just below the left knee. At the time it felt as though she had been kicked by the steel-shod hoof of an angry mule. She fell to the ground clutching at her leg and her hand came away covered in blood. With her strength rapidly fading in shock from the bullet's impact, Abbie had the presence of mind to drag herself back against the wall of the hut and. hauling out the tiny Colt from its location painfully poking her in the small of the back. she stuffed it down into her left moccasin boot.

She lay there sick from the bullet wound and also by the fact that she at long last had been felled by one of the deadly leaden messengers that she had so often sent on their way. The bandits surged forward and for a moment Abbie had the vain hope that she would be overlooked in the dark shadows along the base of the wall. It was not to be. There were excited cries and soon a number of bandits – some of Mexican ancestry, others probably of white origin while yet others were undoubtedly Indian – were gathered around gazing down curiously at the white woman who stared back defiantly up at them.

One tentatively poked at her with the bare toe of a sandal-shod foot. Another followed his example, only harder, and soon others were also kicking at the victim. Initially the blows did not hurt Abbie unduly but she realized that if it continued and increased in intensity she stood a very good chance of being kicked to death.

Suddenly, a harsh, authoritative voice broke in upon their enjoyment, causing the bandits to fall back obediently as a burly figure, his features shadowed in the moonlight, pushed his way through the throng and rapidly gave a series of curt orders, which were immediately carried out.

Abbie's empty pistol was snatched from her hand and given to the leader. Likewise, she was relieved of her gun-belt, holster and her Bowie knife, which in turn were passed to the one giving the orders. He examined them curiously for a brief moment and then issued a further instruction, at which point Abbie found herself picked up in a none too gentle fashion and carted along surrounded by a number of loud and gesticulating bandits.

Arriving at a group of buildings, a door was flung open and she was dumped unceremoniously on the bare floor of what had once been the cell of one of the long-deceased Franciscan fathers. The bandits left the tiny room. The heavy door was slammed shut and Abbie was left alone in her pain and misery.

Abbie wriggled and, sitting herself against the wall, she considered her position. The little cell was about 10ft long by 6ft wide and no doubt had at one time contained a small wooden bed and the sparse posses- sions of the Franciscan. Now there was nothing. High up on one wall was a narrow window space devoid of glass but which permitted a certain amount of light to enter her prison.

Abbie rolled up the leg of her buckskin pants since her next task was to determine the amount of damage done by the bandit's bullet. There was a hole on the right side of her left calf where the ball had entered and another larger hole on the outside of the leg where the missile had exited. From both wounds a small quantity of blood was flowing, though Abbie was relieved that the shot had apparently missed splinter- ing or even hitting a leg bone.

She pulled up her buckskin shirt, thinking of the hours Billy Curtis had spent making the garments, and after much effort succeeded in tearing a long strip from the hem of her chemise. By dint of much rubbing, at length Abbie was able to fray the strip of material into three pieces, two short and one long. She then used the short pieces to plug the holes in her leg, gasping with the pain as she did so and frequently having to stop amid waves of dizziness that threatened to render her unconscious. At last the task was completed and Abbie wound the remainder of the chemise strip around the leg, covering both holes and tying it in a reef knot over the shin bone.

As she gingerly pulled her pant leg down over the wound, she retrieved the Colt from her left boot and tucked it into her waistband, meanwhile considering its limited possibilities. The Pocket model was designed purely for close-counter shooting, being of but .31 calibre and with a 3in barrel and a five-shot cylinder, of which only four chambers were loaded and capped. Abbie knew that, as Billy would have said, 'She had to have an edge,' in order to achieve any success with the limited weapon at her disposal.

As Abbie lay uncomfortably on the cold stone floor trying to ignore the constant throbbing in her lower left leg, she heard noises outside the cell. There were two voices, one a deep male and the other a high-pitched female one in reply. The door opened and a young Mexican or Indian girl entered bearing a bowl of water and some white cloth. These were placed on the floor by Abbie and her visitor went out and returned with a jug of water and an earthenware beaker, which she handed to Abbie with motions for her to drink.

Gladly, Abbie did so, suddenly aware of the fact that

she had a raging thirst. Meanwhile, the girl indicated that she wanted to examine Abbie's wound. Hesitantly, Abbie agreed and nodded her head for the girl to proceed. This she did very gently, easing up the pant leg of the buckskins and carefully removing Abbie's crude first aid attempt, while crooning the while in a soft liquid voice that the English girl recognized as Spanish.

Abbie was determined to try and communicate with her little angel of mercy. 'You are very kind. What is your name?'

Her nurse paused in her act of gently washing the wound. She looked frightened towards the door and raised a finger to her lips, saying 'Ssh!' and then continuing with her ministrations.

Abbie tried again. She pointed to herself. '*Mío* Abbie!' She pointed to the girl, 'You?' she queried.

Again the girl looked towards the door and in a barely audible voice whispered 'Juanita.'

Juanita! Then this girl might well be the Felipe's sister. Abbie decided to probe a little further.

'Juanita is sister of Felipe? Felipe is Abbie's friend!'

The girl looked at Abbie in surprise and whispered, 'Felipe is my brother. *El Caudillo* he tells me Felipe is, how you say, *morte*, dead. *El Caudillo* is a very bad *hombre*, Señorita Abbie. Do not trust him.'

No more was said since a loud voice spoke from outside, from its tone obviously enquiring if Juanita was going to take all day dressing the prisoner's wound. Juanita replied with a small frightened, '*Un momento, señor*,' and hurriedly finishing her bandaging, she gathered the bowl and other things and left the cell.

Abbie was left alone to her own thoughts and she pondered long and hard over the question of 'an edge' with the limited defence weaponry available. After considering and discarding several options, she thought of the way many gamblers were said to produce almost instantaneously a small pistol from concealment in a sleeve. Could she create a similar arrangement?

The sleeves of her buckskin shirt were quite full and, fashioning a crude holster from the discarded material with which she had originally bound her wound, Abbie tied it to her left arm and slipped the little Colt under the binding with the barrel pointing up towards her elbow. All she had to do was slip her right hand inside her left sleeve, grab the butt of the pistol and pull it forth in a sweeping arc. It was crude but was better than nothing.

Jack Harding was fit to be tied by Abbie's non-appearance with the liberated villagers. He questioned Felipe repeatedly about the way in which the operation was conducted and as to what had been the Mexican boy's reaction when Abbie had not fallen back with the two remaining Utes. Felipe for his part described how, after seeing the last of the villagers to safety, he had crept forward in time to see Abbie taken captive and from her movement he believed by all the saints that she was alive.

Dora, seeing Jack standing there in the moonlight

rubbing his chin and scratching his sparse hair, approached and demanded, 'Well, Jack Harding? You're in command now! What are you going to do to rescue Abbie?' She paused and would have continued in similar vein but Jack turned to her and growled.

'Be quiet woman! Let a man think!'

Dora fell silent and Jack pondered the situation while simultaneously roughing out a plan of attack. Finally, he came to a decision and called the members of the column together.

'All right, listen carefully. As most of you already know Abbie was taken captive during the raid to help the villagers. So we have to go in and rescue her. This is what we'll do.

'Jeb!' pointing to one of the men delegated to lead twenty riflemen, 'You'll go with your twenty and take up position east of the village but within rifle range. Cover may be sparse so pick your positions carefully. You'll have the advantage of having the sun behind you, while the bandits will be in direct sunlight with the sun in their eyes. Get into position now but don't open fire until you hear shooting from the north.' Jeb nodded and, motioning to his squad, left the meeting.

Jack turned his attention to Wilf Bateson. 'Wilf, you move forward with Ole Betsey and the rest of your gun team together with the other men I give you until you're in point-blank range. Aim at the old mission buildings because that is where the gang are head-quartered. The rest of you people will form a skirmish line either side of the cannon and will move forward well spread out after the first three cannon shots. Is that clear?'

There were nods and muttered sounds of agreement and the remainder of the night was spent having a hasty meal and checking that all their weaponry was loaded and ready. Some few attempted to grab a little sleep. Others engaged in small talk trying to forget what was to come; one little group had an impromptu prayer meeting and others just waited for the dawn.

In her little cell Abbie also waited as light began to shine on the western wall opposite the small window. As the light increased she realized that she was seeing the birth of another day – a day that in all probability might be her last on earth. She felt dirty and scruffy, and after moistening her lips and rinsing out her mouth, she used the balance of the water Juanita had left in the bowl to engage in a hasty toilette, washing her face and hands and combing her fingers through her hair in an attempt to create a parody of order. Her old slouch hat had been flung into a far corner of the cell and, retrieving it, she jammed it down on her unruly curls and awaited the will of the gaolers.

She had not long to wait. As golden sunlight flooded into the cell, there was the tramp of feet approaching and then the cell door was flung open and two heavily armed bandits entered. One burly wide-sombreroed figure beckoned Abbie. 'Come! *El Caudillo* will see you now.'

Abbie, stiff with sitting on the cold stone floor, struggled to her feet and both of the bandits stepped forward and took her under the arms to steady her as she attempted to get some movement into her stiff and wounded leg. 'Thank you, *míos caballeros*!' declared Abbie in part in gratitude for their help but also to see how they would react to such flattery. They both remained mute as they hustled her out of the cell and along what must have once been a cloister. Looking about, Abbie noted that much of the former mission lay in ruins with gaps in the perimeter defence wall. At length her escort halted before a pair of large battered doors guarded by two lounging bandits who displayed little interest in the female prisoner but concentrated more on the cigarillos that they were both smoking.

A hearty rap on the doors and they swung open. Abbie was thrust inside and her two male companions walked her forward and then stepped back, leaving her standing alone facing a large high-backed empty chair. After the glare of the sunlit courtyard, the large room, which had probably been the refectory at the time when the buildings had served a more noble purpose, seemed in semi- darkness but in a short time she had adjusted to the subdued light coming from a series of small arched openings near to the top of the walls to both her left and her right.

After what seemed to have been a long time but in reality was no more than ten minutes, a small arched door in the wall in front of her opened and there appeared the figure of a large man, who walked forward and seated himself silently in the chair facing her. Not a word was said as captor and captive surveyed each other.

Abbie observed a round-faced swarthy man with

thick lips, much of which were covered by an unkempt black moustache, the same colour as his greasy-looking long hair peeping out from a red bandanna. He was dressed in a none-too-clean embroidered shirt, open at the neck to show his hairy chest, a Mexican-style bolero and pants decorated with conchos, the latter garment being stuffed into black leather riding boots. She noticed with disdain that the fat fingers that grasped the arms of what had most likely once been a prior's chair were bedecked with rings, once the property of ill-fated Mexican women.

Not a word was spoken. The Mexican stared at Abbie with his reptilian eyes until she felt she was being examined as though she was some alien specimen in a laboratory. He saw standing before him a slightly built female with brown tanned features and with her short hair simply tied with a piece of rawhide. He noted the buckskin pants discoloured down the left leg where she had been wounded and her leather shirt rounded by the thrust of her small breasts. She raised her chin and looked back at him defiantly.

'So!' he declared. 'You are the Señorita Pinfire. What do they call you? I am *El Caudillo*!' He emphasised this by striking himself on the chest with his right fist.

Abbie had long decided that she had to display a poise of being superior to this uncouth, uneducated bandit and therefore with head back she looked down her nose at her interrogator and replied. 'You may address me as Ma'am. I do not intend to furnish you with any of my personal information.'

El Caudillo sprang to his feet and shouted, 'You will tell me what I want to know. I am the Chief here. I could have you stripped naked and beaten or handed over to my men. You will answer my questions. I am *El Caudillo*.'

'No you are not *El Caudillo*. In actual fact you are Benito Gomez of Nogales in the province of Sonora. You were being hunted in your country by the Rurales for robbery and more especially for the brutal murder of several people, including your own wife. Now you and your gang of fellow cut-throats are being hunted on both sides of the border.'

Gomez felt that he was losing control of the questioning of the prisoner and changed tack in an attempt to re-establish command of the situation.

'I think, young woman, that you had better learn some respect very quickly. If my friend Bart Bradshaw were here he would not waste time talking politely to you, he would ...' The remainder of his sentence was lost as Abbie went into peals of loud laughter.

'Mr Bradshaw and all of his men would have to come back from the grave to be here, Señor Gomez! They are dead and buried! Every one of them!'

Gomez sat back in his chair, his head in a whirl, Bradshaw dead? Impossible! The little *gringa* bitch was lying to him. Well he'd show her who was the man who gave the orders around here. Enough of this bandying of words. He decided that a glass of wine was in order, to give himself time to think and also to let the *gringa* stand there waiting. That would show her who is the boss.

'Juanita!' he called imperiously. 'Bring me some wine. Now! Don't take all day about it!'

She responded immediately. The girl was visibly shaking with fear and in her haste to comply with the orders slopped some of the wine as she transferred some of the red liquid from a large jug into the glass held by Gomez.

'You clumsy bitch, now you've spilt wine on my freshly polished boot!' He stuck out his left boot. 'Lick it off or I'll take the whip to you again!' Juanita obediently knelt and proceeded to clean up the spilt wine with her tongue.

Abbie was disgusted and horrified by the way that the Mexican girl was being deliberately degraded by the monster who called himself *El Caudillo*. As Juanita completed her loathsome task and scurried from the room, Abbie said in a voice dripping with sarcasm, 'Benito Gomez! What a great man. A real *caballero*. Such a hero. No wonder the women are falling over each other to offer you their charms. If that is the way you act towards a young defenceless girl, how would you react if one had a gun in her hand and knew how to use it?'

'Ah! I forgot. You call yourself the Señorita Pinfire and have somehow tricked people to believe that you are a *pistolera*, an expert with your gun. Well, let's see how good you really are, Juanita! Bring the gun and gun-belt lying on the table. Make it fast.'

Abbie stood there casually waiting. She had already noted one error on the part of the so-called *El Caudillo*. She had not called herself the Pinfire Lady. Others had given her that sobriquet, but she did not intend to correct the error. Let Gomez find out for himself!

Juanita appeared carrying the gun-belt and hol-stered pistol, and at a gesture from Gomez brought it over to where Abbie was standing. As the Mexican girl handed the rig over, she silently mouthed a warning. Abbie stood holding the holster with her right hand while her left held the belt close to the ammunition pouch.

'OK! Now we will pretend to have a little gunfight. You will put on your gun-belt how you want it but leave the gun in the holster. No tricks now. When we are both ready we will shoot at the jug of wine, which Juanita will have upon her head,' he laughed. 'She is a good girl and will do exactly as I want.'

He gestured to the two bandits who had brought Abbie from her cell and they came forward. Taking the terrified Juanita by the arms, they placed her against the far wall of the refectory and balanced the jug of wine upon her head. They both then hurriedly stepped to one side and moved to the far corner. where they hoped they would be out of the way of stray bullets.

Poor Juanita stood there shaking while large tears rolled down her cheeks. She raised both arms to steady the jug and was immediately ordered to lower them by Gomez with his seemingly playful comment of, 'Now, now, *Chiquita*! We must not cheat! That would not be fair.'

Turning to Abbie he queried, 'Are you ready, Señorita Pinfire? If so Lopez,' indicating one of her escorts, 'will give the word and we will both shoot at the jug. You will only have one round in your pistol, so don't get any funny ideas! We will soon see who is the fastest and the most accurate.'

When Abbie had been handed her gun-belt, she had immediately noted from the weight that the gun did not have a full load of shells and a quick glance verified there was but one round in the cylinder, which upon cocking the pistol would be under the hammer. But was it a fired shell? If so she would be shooting an empty gun! The weight of her ammunition pouch suggested that, given the required few seconds, she could reload the empty chambers. That is if she were given those few precious seconds.

Slowly she strapped on her gun-belt and tied the leather thong at the base of her holster around her left leg. Now, to seek 'the edge'! There was a small table close by and Abbie, deliberately exaggerating her limp, moved to lean against the piece of dark furniture with a muttered comment that she hoped her damned leg would hold out.

El Caudillo was getting impatient with her apparent reluctance to get on with his devilish competition. 'Come, *señorita*! I haven't got all day! Are you ready?'

Leaning against the table, Abbie merely nodded and a moment later Lopez cried out, 'Go!'

Abbie had already made up her mind as to her course of action, The first thing was to save Juanita, so with a lightning-swift draw she pulled the small .30 calibre Colt pistol tied to her left arm and dropped into her familiar crouch, simultaneously swinging to aim at the Mexican, who was still in the act of raising his gun and turning to shoot at her.

'Drop it, Gomez!' she screamed, and when he failed to instantly comply she fired all four rounds at his gun arm and, dropping, pulled the table over while she feverishly loaded her pinfire pistol.

Two of the tiny .31 calibre bullets hit Gomez in the arm, causing him to drop his pistol, and a third went high, ripping a deep furrow across his swarthy features. Screaming with rage and pain, the Mexican stood there clutching his right arm and cursing the *gringa* bitch who had not fallen for his trickery.

With the table providing an inadequate shield, Abbie had just completed reloading while bullets thudded into the heavy furniture when there was a crash and a portion of the roof collapsed into the room. A second shell impacted against the thick north wall and this time the bellow of gunfire was heard together with the crackle of small arms fire, indicating to the Mexicans that the mission buildings were under attack.

At the first pistol shots, Juanita's knees had buckled and she had slipped down the wall with the wine jug landing with a crash beside her. She remained there crouched with her arms covering her head as the shell-fire commenced and totally ignored *El Caudillo*'s command to his followers to evacuate the premises. As the three Mexican bandits attempted to exit with *El Caudillo* in the lead, Abbie rose from behind the table and threw a couple of snap-shots after her guards, one of whom yelped as he received a bullet in the posterior.

The door burst open and in rushed Jack Harding, together with Dora and, of all people, Felipe. All three came over to where Abbie was comforting the weeping Juanita. Felipe immediately took charge of his sister, who was totally bewildered by the pleasant change of circumstances, and meanwhile Abbie, Jack and Dora brought each other up to date.

Jack and Dora described the plan of attack and how the operation had gone like clockwork. The startled bandits had had insufficient time to prepare an adequate defence and had been unnerved by the shells dropping upon their positions. Some had fled but the majority had thrown down their arms and, raising their hands high above their heads, they had pleaded for mercy.

Abbie in her turn told her companions about her captivity and the recent events, resulting in the duel with *El Caudillo*. 'Now if we can catch Gomez and the other fugitives we can bring this campaign to a close. Otherwise in a few months we'll have to do the whole operation again.'

Hardly had Abbie completed this last statement than she became aware of a strange, unpleasant sensation as the room around her started going up and down and then moving with increasing rapidity from right to left. She stood clutching the edge of the overturned table and was suddenly embarrassed by a vile sickness as she threw up the contents of her last meal, before lapsing into a state of unconsciousness.

CHAPTER SEVEN

She lay comatose for several days, being tenderly nursed by Dora, Juanita and several of the village women, all of whom had returned to their dwellings. Jacob Levy had the most medical knowledge in the party and he suggested that Abbie's condition was the result of not having her bullet wound attended earlier. Under his direction, a piece of boiled cloth soaked in alcohol was passed through her bullet wound from entry to exit, ensuring that the wound was clean. Then both holes were sewn up but not completely since he stressed that the wound must be allowed to, as he put it, 'weep' before closing of its own accord.

Meanwhile, Jack organized affairs at the mission. The twenty or so bandits who had perished in the assault on their stronghold were buried, as were two of the attackers and the Ute Indian who had participated in the initial raid to free the villagers. Those bandits who had surrendered were sent off to Santa Fe under a strong armed escort to be turned over to the United States Army to stand trial for their misdeeds. Roped neck to neck, the dejected line of captives stumbled past a jeering jubilant line of cheering villagers, while either side of the involuntary marchers there rode a number of hard-eyed watchful victors determined that the bandits would eventually reach their destination and receive justice.

Jack chose ten of the more responsible-appearing villagers and organized them into a town guard, arming them with some of the weapons surrendered by the bandits. Assisted by Felipe, he gave them some basic instruction in the use of the guns at their disposal and ensured that each man could load his weapon and hit a mark at a reasonable distance.

While these affairs were being organized, he and the remainder of the expedition worried and fretted over Abbie's condition. She lay motionless for several days, her forehead bathed in sweat and continually wiped with cool damp cloths. The women had removed all of her dirt- and sweat-stained clothing and tenderly washed her down before dressing her in a long soft cotton robe that could easily be removed for her daily wash.

Jacob insisted it was important that Abbie receive some daily nourishment in the form of a thin gruel and later mixed with some finely chopped cooked meat. That and a spoonful of red wine formed her daily intake for more than a week, and still she lay motionless.

Gradually, as her temperature dropped back to normal, the persistent sweating diminished and she seemed to be in a more restful sleep. Finally, a full two weeks after the shoot-out in the refectory, Abbie opened her eyes and slowly looked about her wonderingly. Her buckskin clothing and her underthings, cleaned and neatly folded, were piled on a chair beside her bed, and her gun-belt and holstered pistol hung on the same chair. Abbie struggled to sit up but for some strange reason found that she did not have the strength to do so.

In a quavering voice that did not seem to belong to her, Abbie called out. 'Is anybody there?'

There was an immediate response and Dora and Juanita rushed into the room, overjoyed that their patient had recovered consciousness but insistent that she lay quietly with the pillows merely tucked up a little so she could see more than just the ceiling.

There followed a short period of convalescence as Abbie took more solid food and attempted to regain her strength. Being a young healthy woman, it was not long before she was sitting on the side of her bed semi-dressed and listening to Jack's report of events and steps taken while she had remained comatose.

Within two weeks, Abbie was up and about, walking to strengthen her leg muscles, eating to gain back some of the weight lost due to her sickness and secretly strapping on her gun-belt and dry-shooting her pinfire pistol.

Two days later, Abbie led the small party of riders that headed out of the abandoned mission of La Cruz in pursuit of Benito Gomez and any of his surviving followers. Jack Harding and Dora, and indeed many others, maintained that she should not be riding yet and that she had done more than her fair share but Abbie was adamant that she was going to resume the hunt.

Jack, in particular, wanted to accompany her but she insisted that he lead the column back and handle affairs at the ranch. For her party, Abbie chose Felipe for his knowledge of Spanish, the remaining two Indian braves of the three who had accompanied her into the village and Minny the Ute girl. From the many volunteers clamouring to go, Abbie selected four single men, all of whom worked for her at either the ranch or the mine and all were proficient with both pistols and rifles.

Well armed, well provisioned, well mounted and with a string of spare horses, they set out at dawn with the cheers and well wishes of the remainder of the column echoing in their ears.

As they rode between the sand dunes, traces of the fleeing bandits became evident, even though a month had elapsed. In their anxiety to avoid capture, the bandits had shed anything that hindered their escape and the pursuers began to note articles of clothing, broken sandals, headgear and even abandoned weapons littering the trail. Then they came upon played out horses that tried to attach themselves to Abbie's party and carcasses of animals, in many cases picked clean by the ever-present vultures. There were also human remains of bandits who, being wounded in the assault, had been left to die of thirst and exposure by their more fortunate companions. The trail divided, with the main body of fugitives heading due south while there were faint indications that a small party had headed eastwards toward the edge of the Staked Plain.

Since it was early evening, Abbie's party made camp and she sent one of the Utes ahead to see if there was any sign of the fleeing bandits on the southern trail. Little Wolf returned shortly before midnight and, waking Abbie, he rendered his report in broken but intelligible English.

'Bandits all caput, Boss Lady. Comanche,' and he drew his hand across his throat and acted out the process of removing a scalp. 'All are dead but I saw no *El Caudillo* among them.'

Both Abbie and Felipe had described the appearance of the bandit leader, so they were certain that Little Wolf's report was accurate. Abbie thought over the implications of the Ute report.

'This suggests that the bandits split up and Gomez and others left the main body and are heading east.

'We'll follow that trail in the morning. Now, apart from the people designated for guard duty, let's get a decent sleep.' And so saying, Abbie turned over in her blankets and tried to set a good example.

Unfortunately, her attempts at sleep did not meet with much success. Her left leg still bothered her and there was a dull persistent throbbing that she tried to ignore. So Abbie lay there wondering if perhaps she had made a mistake for insisting that she would lead the pursuers. Was it merely her pride and the sense that if she had turned over command to another she was somehow losing the magic touch that had made her so successful in the past? These thoughts and many others kept her brain active, and it was almost with relief that Minny came over and shook her saying; 'Coffee Abbie. All mens are get up.'

Abbie sat up in her blankets and discovered to her embarrassment that she was the last person to stir. At first she was unreasonably angered that she had been allowed to sleep on but then her common sense took over as she realized that every one of the patrol was merely being considerate of her weakened condition. With an unspoken nod of thanks, a mug of scalding hot coffee and a biscuit, she was ready to face the trail once more.

CHAPTER EIGHT

They headed east with their assorted headgear pulled down low over their eyes, each squinting to avoid the fierce glare of the angry sun rising before them. They rode silently, each occupied with his own thoughts, bandannas pulled up over their mouths and nose in a vain attempt to avoid the choking dust caused by the passage of their horse hoofs through the powdery surface.

Abbie spotted a shape lying some short distance from the left-hand edge of the faint trail. She called a halt and two of the hands dismounted and checked the body. The sand had drifted against him and since he was lying on his face with arms outstretched as though appealing against his awful lonely fate, his features were still recognizable, though the buzzards had removed most of the flesh from the back and both legs.

It was with mixed feelings that Abbie identified the body as being one of her escort when she was taken to meet with *El Caudillo*; the same one she had wounded with a snap-shot when the ex-leader and his confederates hurriedly exited the refractory. Undoubtedly being wounded, and therefore a burden, his callous companions had left him, probably taking his horse when they did so. Abbie was mortified that she had been the instrument that had led to this poor wretch's lonely death but then she recalled how he had laughed as he insisted that poor Juanita stand still and stop shaking the wine jar perched on her head, and a half-remembered passage from a long forgotten sermon by the regimental chaplain came to mind: 'As ye sow, so shall ye reap.' With that thought, she dismissed her momentary remorse and set her mind to the task ahead.

As the posse travelled eastward, the terrain began to change with the desert giving way to rolling grasslands, sparse at first but becoming more plentiful as the miles passed. Hank, one of the ranch hands, observed that they appeared to be entering cattle country and thought that very soon they would probably be encountering signs of habitation.

Hank was not mistaken. Far off on the eastern horizon, nestled in a hollow between gently rising hills, was a group of buildings that, as they drew nearer, could be seen as a sod-roofed ranch house, a small barn with a corral, another shack and the ubiquitous outhouse.

There was an ominous silence about the whole place. No dogs heralded their approach. There was no smoke curling up from the iron chimneypiece projecting above the weed-covered sod roof and the sound of their hoofs brought nobody out to the porch of either the main building, the barn or the other shack.

'Hullo the house!' Abbie called. 'Anyone here?'

There was no reply to her query. She and her companions remained mounted as they looked around, their hands hovering over gun butts, concerned that they might be the target of a trap. When several minutes had elapsed, Abbie ordered all to dismount and search the area for any sign of the owners.

She and Felipe approached the door of the ranch house and were immediately aware of the persistent buzzing of hundreds of flies going about their work. Pushing wide the half-opened door, they both stepped inside and were brought up short by the scene of horror confronting them.

A grey-haired man sat slumped in a chair with dried blood on his shirt front originating from the two bullet holes in the area of his heart. Close by on the floor lay the body of a younger man, fair-haired by the looks of him, although much of his head was missing due to a shot evidently fired at extremely close range by a large-gauge shotgun. From the condition of the corpses the murders had taken place not more than two or three days prior to the posse's arrival.

As Abbie, kerchief held to her nostrils in a vain attempt to avoid the foul odour, looked around the room for evidence of the victims' identity, Felipe moved into the small room adjacent to the living room. He hurriedly returned, ashen-faced.

Abbie stepped towards him and he raised an arm across the threshold. 'Señorita Abbie, you do not want to go in there!'

Abbie protested. 'Come, Felipe! Could anything be really worse than the sight of those poor men cruelly done to death in their own home?'

She gently pushed the Mexican boy to one side and entered the bedroom, only to be stopped short in utter revulsion. A young woman lay in the double-size bed. Her wrists were tied to the headboard and a rag was stuffed in her mouth. She was bare below the waist, and from the position of her legs it was obvious that she had been raped, no doubt repeatedly. And then the poor creature had had her throat cut from ear to ear.

'Oh, dear God! Who could have done such a wicked thing?' Abbie stood there trembling with rage and with tears starting in her eyes as she stood frozen with the thought of the agony that this young girl must have experienced.

The horror was not yet ended. In a home-made cot on the far side of the bed lay the body of a small infant, not a mark upon the little body but his end was obvious. Abandoned in the house of death, it had no doubt succumbed due to lack of nourishment after the murder of its mother.

Abbie stumbled from the room and into the open, taking great gulps of fresh air in an attempt to rid her lungs of the noxious odours in that ranch house. She cleared her lungs but it would be a long time before she would ever erase the scenes of the atrocities that she had witnessed.

As Abbie stood there, chest heaving, there was a shout from a couple of the men who had been searching the barn and they emerged holding a small, struggling, obviously terrified, figure of a boy, who cried and pleaded with his captors in voluble Spanish.

Abbie turned to Felipe. 'You had better handle this, Felipe. See if you can calm that little fellow down and just maybe we can find out what happened here.'

Felipe nodded and hurried over calling, '*Hola, mí caballero.* What do they call you?'

The struggles ceased and a very dirty, tear-stained face looked up at Felipe and, apparently liking what he saw, volunteered the information he was called Pepito. Felipe reached into his pack and produced a tortilla, which he handed to the boy. Pepito tore at the food ravenously and Felipe, Abbie and the rest of the posse waited patiently until he had finished eating and drinking from a proffered canteen.

'Well, Felipe, what's his story?'

Felipe spoke to Pepito in Spanish and the boy went into a detailed description of his experiences, too fast for Abbie and the other Anglos to grasp more than a word here and there. Finally, the lad finished speaking and looked up at the surrounding adults apprehensively.

Felipe gave Abbie a concise version of Pepito's account. The owner of the ranch was a Mr Wolfgang Reitz and he and Maria, his wife, had taken Pepito in when they found him wandering along the trail the previous year. So he had lived with the Dutch couple for several months, doing little jobs and in general making himself useful. The household had been increased, first of all when Mr Van Ryan, Maria's father, joined them, and then when Maria had given birth to a baby. All had been well and there was no discord at the ranch until the two Mexicanos had arrived. They had told Mr Reitz that they were looking for work and were down on their luck. Mr Reitz didn't really need more hands but, being a soft-hearted man, had agreed to let them stay for a while and they could work for their food and a few dollars. That had been about three or four weeks ago.

Pepito did not like the two strange Mexicans. First of all they came from the north, where there was just desert. Secondly, they treated him like dirt and would cuff him or kick him if the Reitzs were not around. And finally he was suspicious of the fact that they had been wearing guns when he first saw them on the northern trail but when they arrived at the ranch they were unarmed.

Finally, the awful day had arrived. Pepito was out beyond the corrals when he heard Mrs Reitz scream and moments later there were several shots, followed by still more screaming. When he had heard the first scream, Pepito wanted to help the *señora* but he was afraid and instead crept into a secret hiding place out on the rocky hillside where he thought the bad men would not find him. And there he had remained, distinctly hearing the screams and pleas from Señora

Reitz, and then there was silence.

Pepito considered leaving his refuge but was cautious, which was just as well as later he heard one of the men calling his name and he was sure that they were trying to coax him to reveal himself. So he stayed hidden.

Much later there had been one more shot and finally he had emerged and crept into the barn, where he had remained hungry and thirsty until discovered by the posse.

Abbie ordered that the four bodies in the ranch house be wrapped in blankets and selected a small knoll for their final resting place. One of the men who was handy with a whittling knife volunteered to carve headboards for the graves using the information furnished by Pepito and verified by the data shown on the flyleaf of a large family Bible found thrown on the floor of the bedroom.

The murdered family were laid to rest in a simple frontier ceremony attended by all, whites, American and otherwise, Utes, and Mexicans. And over the graves Abbie swore an oath that she would not stop until the perpetrators received justice. Her words were echoed by the remainder of the posse and each person was practically positive that the atrocity had been carried out by Benito Gomez, the late *El Caudillo*.

Their assumptions were reinforced as they were gathering their stock in readiness to hit the trail. Behind the water-trough on the far side of the largest corral was found the body of a man who had been shot in the back He lay face downwards with his arms reached out ahead of him. Nobody had moved the body when Abbie came on the scene and she immediately noticed one curious feature. A large arrow was scratched in the sandy soil pointing in the direction that the corpse was laying, and by the arrowhead was also scratched a large cross. When the body was turned over Abbie recognized the features as those of Lopez, one of the men who had escorted her from her cell to meet *El Caudillo*.

Obviously the latter did not want anyone to associate him with the defeated bandit leader and had therefore callously shot his one remaining follower to eliminate the remaining evidence associating him with La Cruz. But what had Lopez been attempting to tell anyone who stumbled upon his body? One after another, various members of the posse hazarded their guesses as to the meaning of the symbols.

Most agreed that Lopez was attempting to give the direction taken by his killer, but why the cross?

It was Abbie herself who solved the conundrum. She recalled that at the burial Felipe and the other Mexicans had made the Sign of the Cross at the end of the short prayer, Sign of the Cross, a visual statement of belief in the Holy Trinity. Trinity! What was the Spanish term for the Trinity? *La Trinidad*!

'Felipe, is there a town or village south of us called La Trinidad?

'*Sí*, Señorita Abbie, I have heard of such a place but have never been there.'

Abbie made a swift decision. 'Everybody saddle up

72

and prepare to move out. We're heading south to this Trinidad. Fred and George! Put Lopez' body in the ranch house and burn the place, I doubt whether anyone would want to live there. And then catch us up on the trail!'

CHAPTER NINE

Several hours later, the posse had put more than twenty miles between them and the site of the Reitz massacre. The sun was beginning its slow descent to the western horizon when a compact group of riders was spotted coming north towards them. Abbie ordered her posse to spread out so as to present less of a target and they rode cautiously forward with their hands hovering near their guns.

When about 100 yards separated the two groups of horsemen they simultaneously halted and then Abbie, following the example of a tall bronzed man of the northbound riders, urged her horse forward and halted when less than twenty feet from the stranger. He was dressed in range rig with a wide slouch hat pushed back on his forehead. He saluted.

'Good afternoon, Ma'am. Captain McHugh's the name, fourth detachment Texas Rangers. May I ask you who you are and where you're going?'

Abbie smiled at this gravely toned representative of Texan law and suddenly realized that she and her posse were possibly in conflict with local regulations.

'Well Captain! I'm Captain Penraven, first name Abbie, appointed to command this posse from Colorado City. We have been hunting down the bandits who raided ranches and communities up in our area.'

McHugh looked at Abbie and raised his eyebrows in polite disbelief. 'You're leading this posse, Ma'am? First of all may I suggest that down here we normally have a man doing a man's job? Gunplay is no work for a lady! Secondly, you're now in Texas and therefore it's our state organisation, the Texas Rangers, that is responsible for law and order, not self-appointed posses, which frequently end up in trouble and then we have to save their skins!'

Abbie tensed as she listened to his disparaging remarks and silently told herself to cool down as the Ranger continued. 'Lucky we found you, Ma'am, as you may have got yourself in one hell of a fix, begging your pardon, Ma'am. It's fortunate that you came this far south without problems as there is one large bandit gang operating out of an abandoned mission north-west of here and Lord knows what would have happened to you if you had run in with that bunch!'

Abbie laughed and enquired sweetly, 'Tell me, Captain, would that be the gang led by a man who calls himself *El Caudillo*?'

'Why yes, Miss Abbie, if I may call you that? Yes. Have you heard of him?'

'I think, Captain, we had better dismount and order our respective groups to make camp. I have a lot of information to impart to you.' And Abbie signalled back to her posse to relax and make camp, a move that was echoed by the Rangers.

Later, as Abbie sat nursing a welcome mug of coffee produced by Minny, Captain McHugh came over and, after accepting a drink of the hot sweet liquid, suggested a trifle abruptly that he would like to hear what it was that his hostess had to say.

'Well!' Abbie began and then paused looking at the Texan with a half-smile. 'I think that you should know that the outlaw gang of La Cruz at the old abandoned mission, no longer exists. We wiped them out except for a few stragglers who have been hunted down. The only one remaining at large is Benito Gomez himself, who called himself *El Caudillo*, and we know where we think that he is heading.

'Captain, perhaps I had better start at the beginning.' Abbie quickly glossed over her exploits and various gunfights, merely describing leading the wagon train to Colorado City, the attack of the bandits and the subsequent experiences of her column of eighty men and women and the role played by the cannon in dislodging the outlaws from La Cruz. She ended her tale with the events of the last few days, ending with the sad story of the gruesome fate of the Reitz family and her knowledge of the perpetrators.

As Abbie ended her account to a now more than slightly bemused Ranger, one of his men, a sergeant, arrived from their camp. He saluted his commanding officer and was preparing to render a report when he noticed the lady sitting there so quietly. His jaw dropped open and, forgetting himself, he burst out with, 'Holy Mackerel! It's the Pinfire Lady! I saw you at Bent's Fort when you faced Paul LaRue!'

He turned to McHugh, speaking excitedly with the words just tumbling out. 'You should have seen it, Cap'n. She was cool as ice water. Put two slugs into his black heart so close you could cover 'em with a dollar! An' that ain't all.'

He was quite prepared to go on at great length detailing Abbie's gunfighting exploits but she raised one hand and brought his flow of laudatory phrases to a halt. 'Sergeant, I don't believe that Captain McHugh really wants to hear my life story just now. We have more important things to discuss,' and the sergeant, apologizing for his interruption, rendered his report to McHugh, saluted and left.

A perplexed Captain McHugh looked at Abbie in amazement, pulling at his moustache as he digested the information he had received from his sergeant, 'Well, if that doesn't beat the band! What I've just been told kinda alters things somewhat.' He stared down at the campfire, lost in thought as he considered the situation. Finally, he thought of a solution.

'Miss Abbie! Or should I call you Captain Penraven. How would you like to be a temporary member of the Texas Rangers? As such you could legally swear in your posse to assist you in the hunt for Benito Gomez.'

Abbie thought for a moment and decided to accept McHugh's offer since it would legalize their position in Texas, and come to think of it, she recalled that Texans were very sensitive about all matters concerning the

Lone Star State. 'Very well, Captain. I graciously accept your suggestion.'

Both groups of riders were called together and the situation was explained to them. Then Abbie stood before the captain and raised her right hand while her left held a small Bible as she swore an oath that she would uphold the laws and constitution of the State of Texas, after which Captain McHugh stated, 'By the authority invested in me I hereby declare that one, Abigail Penraven, is henceforth a member of the Texas Rangers.'

And with a wide grin, he seized Abbie's right hand and shook it saying, 'Congratulations, Ma'am. You've just made history!'

He produced a five-pointed star engraved with the words 'Texas Ranger' and was just about to pin it on her left breast when the impropriety of such an act prompted him to thrust it at Abbie saying, 'Here! Maybe you'd better pin this on!' The doughty Texas warrior displayed a blush visible through his sunburnt features.

The two groups were dismissed and Abbie and Captain McHugh sat down to plan a concerted campaign. 'Abbie, you say that you believe that Benito Gomez may well have gone to Trinidad. It's quite probable that you're correct in that surmise but tell me, what do you know about Trinidad?'

Abbie confessed that the only member of her posse who had even heard of the place was Felipe, and in his case he had merely overheard confederates of *El Caudillo* mention the place during the period when he was an unwilling gang member.

'Well, Abbie, you might as well know, my orders were to clean out *El Caudillo*'s nest up at La Cruz and if successful I was to take my contingent down and get rid of the Comancheros of Trinidad.'

'Comancheros?' queried Abbie. 'Are they a branch of the Comanche tribe, Captain McHugh?'

'Abbie! The first name is David, commonly called Dave. As one Ranger to another, I guess we can drop the formalities. And in reply to your question regarding these men of Trinidad, no they are not themselves Indians, but a bunch of no-good renegades who have robbed, stolen and murdered in order to trade with the Comanche.

'You should know there are other Comancheros, simple Mexicans and half-breeds, who merely take a few items out into the plains and take the risk of dealing with the Comanche but these ones of Trinidad are most definitely a thorn in the side of the Texan government. We suspect them of robbing ranches and travellers in order to obtain products, clothing, tools, jewellery and weapons, especially guns, with which they trade with the Comanche and also the Kiowa. So, Captain Abbie! We are going to break up their little game and it won't be easy. This is what I propose.'

Dave McHugh suggested that they ride as one column of close on twenty-five riders and upon entering Trinidad they split up into groups of three or four and circulate through the town, making their presence felt.

'This is all very well, Dave, but what about Benito

Gomez? He is our prime reason for being here!'

'I wouldn't worry too much about Señor Gomez. He's a failure and these Comancheros don't take too kindly to one of their ilk who comes among them as a fugitive. In fact he may not even be alive at this very minute.'

CHAPTER TEN

His words were very prophetic. As the column rode down the dusty main and only street in the town of Trinidad, they were greeted by the sight of the face-blackened figure of *El Caudillo*, hands tied behind his back, toes pointing down to the ground as his limp body swung gently in the western breeze. He had been hung from the arm that projected above the upper open door of the livery stable. His fate gave Abbie a shiver as she recalled being faced with a similar end back in Paradise back on the Mountain Division Trail just over a year ago.

Life is very ironic, thought Abbie. There hangs the reason for us coming south from Colorado City. Theoretically we should now be able to turn around and return home. But we've made a further commitment and honour demands that we stick to the bargain made with the Rangers.

Captain McHugh halted his column and, turning, gave his pre-arranged instructions. 'OK Rangers. You can fall out and stretch your legs for a bit. We will assemble by that old adobe church in two hours' time. Fall out.'

As previously arranged, the column broke into small groups of three or four and began to circulate along the main street, some dropping into stores and checking their wares, others sampling the cantinas and saloons, though with strict orders to keep their drinking down to a bare one or two beers. Knowing the Texas attitude towards black and Indian folks, McHugh advised that the Ute braves and Minny remain squatting by the horses, where hopefully they would not be harassed or verbally abused.

Unfortunately this turned out to be wishful thinking on the captain's part. Hardly had the rangers spread out through the town when a small crowd of in the main shiftless saloon barflies began to gather and to make comments about the stoic Indians, who attempted to ignore the ribald and bawdy epithets that were flung in their direction.

Abbie, together with Felipe and Fred and George Lawson, the brothers from her ranch, had gone into a general store and were just looking around fingering the bolts of cloth on the counter and making small purchases of candy and tobacco when one of them heard a commotion coming from the direction of the plaza where their horses were tethered.

Hurriedly paying for their purchases, the four of them made their way back to the plaza to find their Indian comrades were standing hemmed in beside the horses by a gang of shouting jeering men, who pushed at the Utes screaming abuse and spat in their faces while referring to them as butchers and stinkin' scalp-hunters, while their victims merely stood with their arms folded and tried to ignore their persecutors.

As Abbie and the other three reached the scene, one of the bystanders grabbed hold of Minny, crying out, 'Hey fellas! I got me a lil' old squaw! Les' see what she looks like without all that fancy get-up on!' And he ripped her shirt down the front with the intent of totally disrobing her. Minny, her patience long exhausted, pulled her pistol and shot the tormentor in the upper leg. There was a deathly silence among the mob as the other Utes also drew their guns and stood covering the unruly crowd.

'Stand fast everyone!' Abbie's voice rang out. 'Don't anybody make a move because if you do it will probably be the last thing you'll ever do. Now what has happened here?'

The female voice coming from the crowd's left side deflected their attention from the Indians and their drawn guns, and the anger they felt subsided as they saw a chance of more sport. The earlier silence was broken by roars of coarse laughter and ribald comments as, turning, they saw before them the slightly built figure of a young woman dressed in buckskins, wearing the Ranger's tin star and packing a large revolver cross-draw style.

Then the comments became personal observations regarding her and her role. 'Hey look at this, a female Ranger. Don't that beat the band! Quick fellas, better git home or the big bad Ranger'll arrest ya an' throw ya in the hoosegow!'

And it got progressively worse, with suggestions of what individuals would do if they had an hour or two alone with Abbie, coupled with comments as to whether she actually knew how to use the gun she wore.

Finally, one young dandy swaggered out from of the crowd, calling out, 'Come on, lady Ranger! Let's me an' you have a lil' old gunfight. I'll try not to scare you too much!'

As he said this, he turned and winked at his supporters, one of whom called out, 'Go easy on her, Jed. She's likely to wet her drawers any minute now!'

Jed swung back, 'OK. lady Ranger, let's draw! Now!' And he started to pull the Navy Colt he wore low down on his right hip.

Abbie allowed him to half draw his pistol and then reluctantly drew with the lightning-fast movements that had made her notorious in the Colorado territory. Dropping into her familiar crouch, her right hand swept across and pulled her pinfire pistol in one fluid movement, quicker than most of the onlookers could see. As her pistol swung in front of her, the left hand curled around the frame ahead of the trigger guard while her left thumb brought the hammer back as her right forefinger squeezed the trigger.

Jed hadn't even cocked his Colt when the 12mm bullet slammed into his right shoulder, throwing him backwards and causing the gun to drop from his nerveless hand. He lay there terrified with his left hand clutching his shattered right shoulder as Abbie stalked towards him, her smoking pistol held firmly in one hand.

'Well, young man. I think that you'll agree that you may have made a little error of judgement,' and turning to the awe-struck crowd she waved her pistol across them, prompting many to cringe, and ordered them to disperse and to take the other wounded man with them. 'Remember! These Indians are fellow offi-cers (Abbie stretched the truth a trifle here) and an attack on any of them will bring swift retribution. We'll attend to Jed, now go!' And the crowd departed hur-riedly.

She knelt by the wounded Jed and his face grimaced with pain as he sat there in the dust with blood trick-ling down between his fingers. 'Sorry that I had to wing you. I tried to position that shot so that it wouldn't smash any bones but one can't be that accurate all the time. Let's have a look at my work.'

Abbie gently removed his left hand and, drawing her Bowie, slit his shirt to lay bare the wound that she had created. 'Oh that's not too bad, Jed. Is that your name? Now, is there a competent sawbones in town? If so we'll take you to him. If not one of our men will dress the wound.'

Jed Oldberg muttered his thanks and whispered that the only doctor in town would be probably drunk by this time of day. To tell the truth his mind was in a whirl. First he was shot by of all opponents a female gunslinger who, unlike gunfighters whom he had seen or of whom he had heard, didn't stand there crowing and preparing to finish him off but rather seemed gen-uinely concerned about the wound that she had caused and expressed a desire in that strange clipped

English accent to help him.

Their brief conversation was interrupted by the arrival of a short figure in a long hooded cassock.

'Permit me to assist you, *señorita*. My name is Padre Pedro. I am the pastor of that little church of Santa Maria over there. If you would care to bring the wounded boy over to my house I can attend to him since through the years I have cared for many wounded men.'

'Thank you, Padre! We will certainly avail ourselves of your offer.' Abbie turned to Fred and George Lawson, instructing them to remain with the Utes and to see that there was no further incidents, and having checked that Minny was fully recovered from her thwarted assault. Then she and Felipe helped Jed to his feet and, following the padre, they went to his small cottage beside the church. Inside, the groaning boy was lowered onto a long leather couch while Padre Pedro bustled around making preparations to dress the wound.

Abbie and Felipe looked around curiously at the sparse furnishings of the little priest's home. There was a sturdy-looking table and two chairs with a rather worn armchair by an unlit stove. On the wall was a crucifix and a statue of the Madonna in a small niche fronted by a flickering candle. Several book-shelves with a collection of battered volumes and a tall cupboard in one corner, from which the padre brought forth his medical kit, completed their inspection.

To take the patient's thoughts away from the forthcoming medical administration, Abbie engaged Jed in conversation. Having ascertained that his full name was Jedediah Oldberg and that he was eighteen years of age, well nearly nineteen he maintained, she asked him how he came to be in Trinidad and what he did for a living. Jed admitted that he was a drifter. His parents had died in east Texas when he was about fourteen years of age and he had wandered west from town to town picking up odd jobs where ever he could. In his travels he had acquired an old Navy Colt and had practised with it until he thought that he was quite a potential gunfighter. 'But nowhere as fast as you, Ma'am. How the h . . .' he paused, 'Sorry, Ma'am! How the dickens did you ever get so fast an' so accurate with it?'

Abbie smiled and suggested that Jed not worry about her skills with a gun for quite a while but concentrate on getting his shoulder better.

As Padre Pedro came over bearing a bowl of steaming water and bandages, Jed completed their talk by telling Abbie that he'd originally come to Trinidad after learning that there was money to be made here, especially if one was good with a gun.

Abbie and Felipe remained while Jed's wound was being skilfully treated and then, after thanking the little padre for his help, they made their way back across the plaza to where all their comrades, Rangers and posse members had gathered after their two-hour circulation of the town. Most had found the population of Trinidad very tight-lipped and had not discovered any information about the Comancheros and their hide-out. The only significant item was Jed's remark to Abbie that someone was apparently hiring gun hands.

CHAPTER ELEVEN

On their approach to Trinidad, Dave McHugh had noted a good spot for an extended camp with running water, good grazing for the animals and a certain amount of shade from the harsh glare of the noonday sun. Mounting up, they rode in that direction and within a short time had established the outline of a Ranger camp with a designated kitchen area, horse lines and even a demarcated area where Abbie and Minny could perform their toilette in seclusion.

Supper was cooked and eaten, and afterwards pipes were lit as the group lay contentedly smoking and leaning on their saddles. Abbie and Dave had a brief talk about the joint plans for the morrow and, their conversation at an end, Captain McHugh got up and strolled over towards the horse lines.

There came a sudden crack, and a long gout of flame lit up the dark undergrowth on the edge of the clearing. McHugh pitched forward on his face in front of the Appaloosa that he had just brought an evening treat as the sound of galloping hoofs advertised the fact that the would-be assassin was rapidly vanishing in the darkness.

Abbie, together with others, ran forward to where Dave was lying. 'Somebody bring a light here!' was the cry and a lantern was brought. Dave was on his face, both arms outstretched with his hands clutching at the coarse grass. The ball had hit the leather V of his suspenders and had been deflected in a deep furrow across his back and gone under the right shoulder blade. An inch lower and it would have smashed his back bone. As it was, he had sustained a life-threatening wound.

It was decided to get him to Padre Pedro as quickly as possible as apparently he was the only one with the skills to attend to such a wound. As the Rangers prepared a primitive stretcher on which to place their wounded captain, he opened his eyes and called for Sergeant Campbell, the one who had identified Abbie as the Pinfire Lady. 'Sergeant Campbell!' he called out weakly, and when the latter appeared he said, 'Sergeant, in my absence I'm appointing Captain Penraven to command the unit. Have the men obey her as they would me.' And he sank back unconscious on the litter.

Leaving Sergeant Campbell to organize the night camp, with strong advice that all keep out of the campfire light, Abbie accompanied the four men carrying the litter through the town to the priest's house. The dwelling was in darkness and she knocked quietly on the door. After a short silence, Father Pedro opened the door and Abbie whispered her appeal that he tended to their wounded commander.

There was no hesitation. He beckoned to her to bring Captain McHugh in and quickly turned up the wick of an oil lamp standing on the table. The captain was placed on the same couch that had held Jed Oldberg and the little priest prepared to operate for a second time that day.

The five from the camp waited until Father Pedro had extracted the lead bullet and had packed and bound the wound. Abbie insisted on giving the priest an offering over Father Pedro's strenuous objections to pay for anything the captain might need, since it was considered too dangerous for him to be moved. Reluctantly, the little padre accepted Abbie's offering and volunteered the information that Jed had left earlier but had agreed to return and have his wound re-dressed.

Abbie and the others walked quietly back through the silent street to their waiting camp and as she walked along, her thoughts wandered over some of the strange paths she had travelled in her short life.

What would Aunt Sarah have to say about some of the more recent events? She suppressed a girlish giggle as she considered her aunt's probable comment regarding her niece's latest enlistment. 'Oh Abbie, they don't even have a decent-looking uniform!'

The rest of the night proved to be uneventful and at first light Abbie went with two of the Utes to scout the area from whence had come the shot that laid Captain McHugh low. She watched with great interest as the two braves carefully searched every inch of the ground and then, satisfied with their examination, moved away from the camp to a spot where the would-be dry-gulcher had left his horse.

Abbie had discovered the area where the shooter had waited but that was the limit of her finds. Her two companions added far more detail. The man had been short of stature, they said, showing her where the leaves had been burnt at a certain height by the blast of his weapon. He was probably Mexican by the remains of a tortilla thrown in the bushes. He walked with a limp since his foot imprints were uneven and he wore riding boots with a hole in the left sole. One other factor they took pains to explain to Abbie; the shooter must have waited a long time since he had found a need to relieve himself and both braves insisted in demonstrating with sign language where he had stood to urinate.

Abbie fought to keep a straight face and continued to display a solemn mien as befitting a chief and her two followers. She called to Minny to pass on her next instructions. They were to take their horses and follow the trail left by the shooter's steed but to be very careful that they were not observed.

She meanwhile returned to camp and indulged in a welcome cup of scalding hot coffee and a sourdough biscuit. After her hurried breakfast, Abbie took two of the Rangers into town and went to check on Captain McHugh. Father Pedro was absent celebrating mass in the adobe church but she was pleasantly surprised to find Jed Oldberg pottering around in the priest's house and acting as a one-armed male nurse to the wounded ranger.

'Jed Oldberg! I'm really pleased to see that you're up and about. But what are you doing here?'

Jed turned his face away, but not before Abbie had noticed that it was cut and swollen. 'What on earth has happened to your poor face?'

Jed made a feeble effort to explain that he had stumbled and fallen in the dark, when his tale of woe was interrupted by the voice of Padre Pedro coming from the doorway.

'The boy lies, *Señorita Commandante*. He left here and returned to the place where he had been living before yesterday. Ace Lonergan is the one who beat the boy. That big brute is almost twice Jed's size and doesn't have one arm in a sling. Lonergan and maybe some others of Jed's so-called friends left the lad unconscious in the alley. One of my little flock found him and brought him to me. Jed himself won't talk about it but among the peons it is common knowledge.'

Jed stood there, head down, facing the stove with his face in shadow. Abbie went over and put her arm across his shoulders. 'Come and sit down next to me, Jed. Is it true what the Padre has told us? If you have any friends in Trinidad it is us, not that bunch of hoodlums. Start at the beginning and give us the complete story.'

Seated together at the opposite end of the long leather couch where Captain McHugh lay sleeping restlessly, Abbie slowly obtained the story from a reluctant Jed. Despite Father Pedro's pleas, he had decided to leave a short while after his bullet wound had been dressed and returned to the saloon where he had hung out before the affair in the plaza.

To his surprise and dismay, his erstwhile friends cold-shouldered him or alternatively made derogatory comments about his stupidity in challenging a Ranger, even if she was only a woman. Others jeered at him, deriding his pitiful shooting, the lack of speed with which he cleared leather and the sad fact that he didn't get off a single shot. The main point was that he had drawn attention to himself and was no use to their bunch any more.

At that moment Ace Lonergan had entered from a back room and, shouldering the crowd aside, came face to face with a white-faced Jed Oldberg. Ace was livid and trembling with a worked up rage as he described Jed as a dumb farm hick and went on to refer to him and his parents with vile insults, which had finally prompted the boy to swing a wild weak punch while defending their honour. Ace had laughed as he had knocked the blow to one side, exclaiming that Jed had given him a valid reason to lick the tar out of him, which he had then proceeded to do until the unconscious boy was thrown out into a side alley. He was found by Manuel Ortega, who had brought him to the padre.

Abbie made one of her split second decisions. 'Jed, you're coming back with us to the Ranger camp. You could probably stay here with Father Pedro but it wouldn't be fair to him and I suspect that you wouldn't be safe anywhere in town. Unfortunately I suspect that

Lonergan and company believe that you have, or will, pass on information to us and they may decide to silence you for good.'

In vain, Jed was protesting that he didn't, in his words, 'know nothing' to tell the Rangers, when a shot came through the window and smashed into the wall behind the stove, which convinced him that it wasn't healthy for him out on the streets of Trinidad.

One of the Rangers was instructed to remain with Captain McHugh until relieved, while the other would go with Abbie and escort Jed to the Ranger camp.

The trio left the priest's house and walked down the street with Abbie and Ranger Tom Budner walking on either side of the apprehensive lad. Initially all went well but as they approached the saloon where Jed had had his so-called pals, a small crowd gathered on the porch and others pushed their way through the bat-wing doors to join them. Then the cat-calls started, directed at the boy as well as the two Rangers.

A hulking great figure stepped off the porch and confronted them. 'Hey! Where d'ya think you're taking young Jeddy boy?'

In a loud clear voice, Abbie responded, 'He's being taken into protective custody. Though it's none of your business. Get out of the way and let us pass!'

'Hold on now, young woman! Nobody speaks to Ace Lonergan like that. Besides which, it is my business. That boy works for me.'

Jed whispered a fervent, 'No I don't any more. I quit yesterday!' as the trio sidestepped and made as though to walk around the fuming Lonergan.

'Don't take another step or it'll be the worse for you! Jed, get over here!'

Abbie stepped in front of Jed and effectively blocked him from Lonergan. 'Mr Lonergan! Or whatever your name really is. You are becoming more than a trifle tiresome. Why don't you be a good little boy and run along home and play with your toys or something. Off you go now! Shoo!' And Abbie made shooing motions as though driving off a troublesome dog.

Her actions had the desired effect. There was a roar of laughter, which for a short while at least had the porch crowd on her side, while Lonergan stood there feeling ridiculous. Renowned for having a very short fuse, the jeering comments from the boardwalk coupled with Abbie's contemptuous reaction to his attempt to assert his perceived authority provoked the inevitable reaction.

Lonergan exploded into a volley of foul epithets directed at Abbie, the mildest of which referred to her as a 'fatherless Ranger whore!' and thereafter got more and more obscene and insulting. Abbie just stood and smiled sweetly at him, which drove Ace to distraction. He dragged at the holster on his right hip, drawing the Remington .44 that he carried.

By gunfighting standards he was pitifully slow since Lonergan traditionally used his fists and boots to enforce his will. Abbie permitted his pistol to actually clear leather before she drew her 12mm pinfire and put a bullet into his left kneecap, followed by a shot that smashed into his beefy right arm and caused him to drop his pistol.

Ace roared with pain and anger, and made the mistake of hobbling towards his female adversary, whereupon Abbie reluctantly placed her third shot in his right leg, dropping him down into the dirt of the street. With a distinct sense of déjà vu, she walked forward and placed the hot muzzle of her pistol right between his eyes in the middle of his forehead. Like a rabbit hypnotized by a snake, Ace Lonergan stared along the barrel of her cocked pistol, now fully aware that a slight pressure on the trigger could send him into oblivion.

The porch crowd had become silent as the drama unfolded before them in the street and now there were polite murmurings as Abbie spoke quietly to Ace. 'Mr Lonergan, I think that you should get your wounds attended to and as soon as you can travel you get out of Trinidad and find somewhere else to reside, preferably a long way away!'

With that last remark she decocked her revolver and, slipping it into its holster, she turned to her two companions and suggested, 'C'mon let's get back to camp!' As they walked away they could hear Ace pleading for someone to come and help him.

CHAPTER TWELVE

Arriving back at the Ranger encampment, Sergeant Campbell hurried over to report that the two Indian braves who had set out to try and trail the man who had shot Captain McHugh had returned with some interesting news.

Abbie bade them come over and, using Minny to enlarge upon their limited English, listened to their story. The two Indians described how they had tracked the shooter westward for quite some distance and then had lost the trail amid stony ground. They apparently had spent some considerable time casting around in ever increasing circles and eventually were successful in picking up the tracks once more. They described the terrain of low hills with an arid parched soil, not quite desert yet certainly not good grazing. When the two braves noted a thin column of smoke rising lazily in the air they proceeded, slowly and cautiously, and peering over the brow of a rocky outcrop, they were surprised to see in a wide valley a large well-guarded hacienda.

In a mixture of English terms, Pidgin English and sign language, the Utes described a series of buildings that showed signs of having been burned and abandoned in the past but recently renovated.

They had carefully made their way right around the hacienda and were able to sketch an outline in the dirt stressing the fact that both the walls and the gateway had armed guards.

Abbie sat and pondered over this latest information. It was, she felt, imperative that she had a discussion with Captain McHugh to compare views on what she thought was the situation in and around La Trinidad. As she sat mulling things over, there was a shout of 'Hello the camp!' and a party made its way into the light of the campfire.

She was delighted yet concerned to see that the group that had hailed the camp consisted of the Ranger she'd left at Father Pedro's cottage and four peons carefully bearing a litter, upon which was reclining a grinning Captain McHugh. Hurrying over to where the litter was deposited Abbie knelt by his side and, clasping his extended hand, burst out with, 'David McHugh! What on earth are you doing here? You're supposed to be still abed in the care of Padre Pedro!'

Captain McHugh explained that he and the good padre had discussed his condition in great detail and it had been agreed that as long as he rested he would be much safer with his own men, especially considering the shot through the window. 'There seem to be two factions in Trinidad. There are the law and order people led by Padre Pedro and I imagine most of his flock and also probably a sprinkling of some of the Texan townspeople. That's one group. Then there are rowdies led by people like Ace Lonergan who have entirely different motives for being here and indeed there may be yet others who have yet to reveal themselves.'

Abbie nodded in agreement as these had been her thoughts when McHugh had arrived. 'However,' she said. 'I think that the web extends much further than the town.'

She described the Utes' report and called to one of the peons drinking coffee by the fire. '*Señor*, do you know anything about a big hacienda maybe fifteen miles to the west of La Trinidad?'

He was most definitely uncomfortable with her question. He rolled his eyes heavenward and looked around the campsite as though seeking an avenue of escape. Abbie put a hand on his right shoulder and, gripping him firmly, shook him gently, saying, 'Come now, hombre! You are a brave one, otherwise Padre Pedro would not have chosen you to assist the wounded *El Capitán*. What do you know?'

After several false starts, the peon summoned up his courage and told her and Captain McHugh the story of Hacienda Alvarez. Don Casimir Alvarez and his family had settled on a large tract of land granted to them by the King of Spain. For more than 100 years the Alvarez family had lived there and had prospered. Then one awful day the Comanche had attacked in overwhelming numbers. They had captured, looted and burnt the hacienda. None had been spared. Thereafter the location had got a name for being haunted and this story had grown as the years had passed. Strange lights were seen when the hacienda was viewed from a distance and one or two hardy souls had completely vanished when venturing too close. These unfortunates had never been seen again. 'It is a most evil place, *señorita*!' And he fervently crossed himself.

Abbie and David McHugh looked at each other and she was the first to break the silence. 'So! We have yet another factor to be considered. Who is out at the Hacienda Alvarez and why did they take a pot-shot at you?'

'There is another strange thing that must be part of the equation, Abbie. That man Gomez, *El Caudillo*, your posse was chasing. Who finished him off? It would seem that he deliberately came to Trinidad but for some reason he was decidedly unwelcome. Did he meet his end at the hands of the good people of the town, the bad element or the ones who take shots in the dark?'

Their attempts to unravel the mysteries of La Trinidad were interrupted by the arrival of an agitated Mexican riding an unhappy mule. Without dismounting, he passed on a message from the padre that there was yet another body hanging in the street and he called for Rangers to come to the scene of the crime. Abbie looked at McHugh and shrugged her shoulders. 'Well, David, you're hardly in a position to trot into town so I'd better go. I'll take three of my own men with me.'

Five minutes later, Abbie and three of her ranch hands were on the trail back into town. A large crowd was gathered in front of the livery stable staring and whispering at the sight of yet another body hanging from the hoist above the open door. Pushing their horses through the crowd, the quartet dismounted and looked up at the corpse of Ace Lonergan slowly turning round and round in the night air.

Abbie stared up at the corpse in dismay. During her mismatched duel with Lonergan she had had no desire to kill her opponent and indeed had deliberately shot to merely disable him, yet here he was dead and irrationally she felt somehow responsible.

She turned to the crowd and demanded. 'Who amongst you either saw Lonergan's body hung up here or saw the men who did this?' Her call for information was met with silence and the crowd started to drift away. Obviously nobody wanted to get involved.

One of her ranch hands entered the livery stable and, climbing up to the hay loft, untied the rope that had run over the pulley of the hoist and acted as a ready-made gallows to receive Lonergan. The body was lowered and removed on a handcart to the one and only undertaker in town to be prepared for burial. Meanwhile, Abbie made her way to Padre Pedro's cottage and, seeing there was a light in the window, she presumed that he was not yet retired and knocked on the door. A quiet voice in Spanish invited her to enter and she did so apologizing because of the lateness of the hour.

'That is all right, *señorita*. I am an old man and need very little sleep. I seldom get to bed before midnight. What can I do for you?'

'Father, did you hear what happened tonight to Ace Lonergan? In a way I feel partly responsible since I made him vulnerable by wounding him earlier in the evening!'

The priest looked at Abbie sympathetically. '*Señorita*, it is intent that counts. You did not intend to mortally wound him but merely prevent him from injuring others including yourself, and it may ease you to know that Ace was already dead when he was hung. If you examine the corpse carefully I am told that there is a line around his neck where he was garrotted. So I am informed by some of my flock.'

'Thank you for telling me, Padre. That sets my mind at rest. But why on earth was Ace murdered?'

Padre Pedro shook his head. 'Some of my parishioners tell me many things. They confide in me, I mean apart from the confessional. The manner of Lonergan's death came to them as hearsay. Someday one may know enough to tell me why Ace died his horrible death despite the fact that he was no doubt a great sinner. For now there is a veil of silence over the affair.'

Abbie thanked the priest and turned to leave. 'One last thing, Padre, what do you know about the Hacienda Alvarez? Did you ever go there in the days before the Indian attack? Did you know that it is occupied once more and apparently they don't welcome visitors?'

'Ah, the Hacienda Alvarez! Yes I went there in the days before the Comanche raid. Senor Alvarez was a true *hidalgo* of the old school, and the *señora*, she was a lady. They always wanted me to celebrate mass there on their wedding anniversary.' He sighed. 'They were a good family.' He paused. 'Except for Antonio, their son. He was going through a wild phase. But there now, I shouldn't speak unkindly of the dead.' And Padre Pedro smiled sadly.

'Regarding the ruins of the hacienda and the rumours of bad people living there, I have heard these tales and advised my parishioners to keep away from the place. It has an evil reputation and there are many ruthless men living here in west Texas so the stories about the hacienda Alvarez may well be true. If I hear anything I'll try to get word to you.'

CHAPTER THIRTEEN

Abbie left the little priest and joining her ranch hands the four of them rode back to camp, where Abbie sat down with Captain McHugh and related the events from the time that the *peon* had brought word of another hanging.

'While you were in town, Abbie, I did some thinking. My original orders were to investigate Comancheros activity in the La Trinidad area. At the time I thought this would mean in the town proper but since then I've modified my ideas somewhat and I now realize that anywhere in a radius of twenty miles of the town could be described as "in the La Trinidad area". Do you agree?'

Abbie was silent for a moment and then nodded, 'Yes, I'm sure that you are right and I suspect that the Hacienda Alvarez could stand a much closer scrutiny. I suggest that we maintain a twenty-four hour watch on that location!'

McHugh was in full agreement and added a notion

that they send out scouting parties to sweep the countryside beyond the hacienda. It was decided to have two scouting parties: one to maintain and record all activity going on at the Alvarez location, the other to roam further afield. Each party was to consist of a Ute brave, one of Abbie's ranch hands and a Ranger. The latter was to give each scouting group a stronger air of respectability. The hour being late, after designating the men for the scouting groups, Abbie and McHugh sought their individual blankets to seek a short night's sleep.

Initially, Abbie had wanted to go with one of the scouting groups but Captain McHugh had cautioned against the notion. Therefore from the time that the groups rode out until five days later when they reported in, she stalked around the camp, constantly tempted to throw a saddle on her bay but mindful of the need to obey orders like anyone else under McHugh's command.

Finally the time came when a lookout reported riders coming in from the west and a little later stated that he could see six men, which indicated that the two groups had linked up at some point in their return journey.

The men rode in and Captain McHugh and Abbie waited patiently while the scouts, with greetings over, tucked into a hearty camp-cooked meal washed down with copious mugs of hot coffee. Their meal finished, the men settled down on their haunches, drawing on their pipes and Mexican 'seegars', and prepared to render their reports.

Ranger Tom Budner described how they had hid their horses in a deep gully with a trickle of water at the bottom and in four-hour shifts had kept a steady watch on the activities of Hacienda Alvarez. Most of the time, the watch was very boring. Hot and boring, watching the guards on the walls and the one on the gate as the former sauntered along the wall and the latter leaned against the gatepost and leisurely scratched his crotch, 'They all did that, Cap'n! Without fail! Each son of a gun scratched. . . .'

He broke off as McHugh indicated Abbie's presence and suggested that he continue with his report.

Three times they noted the arrival of the two-wheeled Comancheros carts from the south and once a train of four of these set out going north into the region of the Staked Plain. The only other thing they noted was the visit of a man, who was identified as one of the idlers who had egged on Ace Lonergan back in La Trinidad. He came early on the second morning and left by midday, heading back on the same grey mule on which he had arrived.

Abbie commented, 'So it seems that someone at Hacienda Alvarez is getting a regular report on what goes on in town!'

Captain McHugh turned to the second Ranger, Wilson. 'OK Bill, let's hear how your scouting party fared.'

Wilson puffed on his pipe and then commenced his report. 'Well sir, we cast a series of searches from east of the Hacienda south and west so we were covering a huge semicircle. The first one was about a mile from the building and we gradually extended the distance so eventually we were due south of the camp here when we started our last sweep. The strange thing, Sir, is that there are no other occupied houses, ranches or even huts in the area we covered. The only living human beings that we saw were two men driving those empty Comancheros' carts south on the first day. We were about to head back to camp when ole' Buck here (he indicated the Ute brave who had been part of his scouting group) saw carts in the distant south coming north. He was certain they were driven by the same men but now the carts were apparently heavily laden so we trailed them.

'Both drivers seemed to have had a skin-full from the way that they shouted and even sang to each other. I guess they didn't want to arrive at the hacienda in that condition 'cos they pulled off the trail and, staggering more than a little, made camp about three miles south of their destination. When we were sure that they were dead to the world, Buck checked out the contents of their carts, an' what do you think he found?'

Bill looked at Abbie and his captain with a grim smile on his face. Since neither ventured to hazard a guess as to the carts' cargo he continued, 'Clothing, ladies' mostly, dresses and other more personal stuff, pots and pans and other household goods and guns, mostly flinters with the odd percussion weapon. Buck says that the whole cargo smelt of blood. Here! Take a look at this!' Reaching into a saddle-bag, Bill produced a piece of clothing, which he handed to McHugh, who took it and after a quick examination passed it silently to Abbie.

She opened it up and saw that it was a blouse, low in the neck laced with a drawstring. Originally, like so many she had seen before, it had been white but now the colour was marred with a huge, rust-like stain down the front. The rust was undoubtedly dried blood and Abbie's thoughts went out to the young Mexican girl who had probably been wearing the garment when her life was ended.

She stared at McHugh, horror-stricken with the thoughts of the suffering that had created two carts of personal goods. 'What does it mean, David?'

He looked at her grimly. 'I suspect that below the border in Chihuahua province isolated haciendas are being raided and probably wiped out to provide such cart loads. But who, and why? Those are questions that need answering.' A thought struck him. 'Where's that young lad Jed that you wounded when we first arrived?'

Someone called for Jed Oldberg to report to the two leaders and he came over from where a group of rangers were sitting yarning.

Captain McHugh invited him to sit or squat, whichever was more comfortable. 'Jed, when you came to Trinidad and were preparing to ride with Ace Lonergan and his bunch, what were you told?'

Jed thought for a moment 'Well sir. As you probably know I'd made out that I was a hard case and was on the dodge after some lethal gunplay further east. It wasn't true!' he hastened to add. 'Well Ace told me that the men chosen had to be good riders and more

109

than good with both pistols an' long guns. Once hired there would be no turning back. Once accepted there would be no backing out. We would be expected to obey orders whatever they were without question and be ruthless if need be. The pay would be good and chances were we could make more on the side. Ace didn't really explain more than that. The reason that he beat me up was because he said that I was showing off and drawing attention to myself, which was bad especially with you Rangers in town.'

'Oh!' Jed hastened to add. 'Some knowledge of Spanish would help as we would be riding south. I guess that's all.'

He was dismissed and Abbie remarked that it was a good thing that she'd shot the boy and therefore saved him from entering a life of crime.

McHugh agreed with her observation and went on to sum up what they had learned from Jed and the scouts. 'So Abbie! The situation appears to be this. Isolated homes south of the border are being raided and the occupants murdered by a gang of scallywags operating probably from the north of the Rio Grande. The proceeds from these raids are being brought north to a rebuilt hacienda and then apparently used for trading with the native tribes such as the Kiowa and the Comanche.'

'Trading for what, David? The tribes you've mentioned don't engage in industry!'

'No, but they do have access to both gold and silver deposits. Braves have often been seen to wear gold to enhance their finery. But they will never reveal the source of the metal.'

Thinking back over what Jed had told them, Abbie mused, 'So that is probably why Lonergan was murdered. He knew too much but was of no further use to whoever is heading this gang, so therefore he was silenced.' She shuddered. 'What an awful inhumane philosophy!'

'You'e right, Abbie! Somehow we have to break up this group but where to start. I can barely walk and you are. . . .' Captain McHugh paused in confusion as despite Abbie's well-recorded ability to lead and command in action his whole training to date suggested that as a woman her powers were far more limited than those of a man.

Abbie rose to her feet and stood looking down at him with arms akimbo 'Now you look here, David McHugh! I can sense what you were about to say and before you utter a single word let me state that you're wrong. I'll lead a force against these villains and you won't regret my commanding such a unit!'

'Very well, Abbie! Let's hear your plan of campaign!'

Abbie was silent for several minutes and Captain McHugh wondered if she was already regretting her outburst. In reality, Abbie was thinking hard and formulating her plans while discarding other notions.

Finally, she raised her head and said, 'Right! This is what I propose. First we send Felipe to Padre Pedro to see if a message can be sent to the Mexican authorities in Chihuahua, possibly the local Rurales, explaining the situation and encouraging them to take action themselves against these raiders.

'One of the major things we should do is to obtain reinforcements. If we have to attack that hacienda we are going to need more men. I'll send a note to my ranch foreman, Jack Harding, instructing him to raise a flying column of say, twenty more well-armed riders and bring them down to Trinidad post-haste. It might be a good idea for him to also bring along Wilf Bateson and his gunners. The bark of a field piece is frequently a great inducement for people to surrender.

'During the time that these forces are gathering, I'll take a posse south following the trail of the carts and hopefully we can locate the hide-out of the raiders – if they are on the American side of the border. If so we'll engage them and, if they don't surrender, we'll wipe them out! Or at least ensure that none get word back to the hacienda.'

CHAPTER FOURTEEN

Early the following day, two riders headed north. One was one of Abbie's ranch hands. He was accompanied by one of the Ute braves. Both were well armed and each had a spare horse. Their orders were to get up to the ranch as quickly as possible, hard riding by night and day, to deliver the message for an additional posse to come south to the ranger camp near Trinidad.

Meanwhile, Abbie chose the twelve men who were to accompany her south to seek out and destroy the nest of the raiders. After due deliberation and consultation with Captain McHugh, she selected eight of the veteran rangers; Fred and George Lawson from her own ranch and the two remaining Ute braves.

After an impassioned plea in a mixture of broken English, voluble Ute and sign language, she included Minny the Ute girl, who by this time had become quite adept with a pistol under Abbie's tutelage.

The punitive column rode out in the mid-morning

heading east. Abbie wanted to lull the suspicions of any watchers that their intent was not to be riding either towards the hacienda or to the south of Trinidad. The remainder of the mixed group left in the camp were instructed to mill around to give the impression that the numbers present had not decreased.

When they were several miles east of the town and were assured by a Ute scout that the column was not being trailed, they swung south, keeping to stony ground as much as possible to increase the difficulty of any would-be pursuers.

Finally, in mid-afternoon, the column swung west to eventually cut the trail of the Comancheros' carts going to and from the hacienda towards the border. Since the cart tracks had been partly covered by the drifting sand it seemed apparent that they were ahead of the drivers making the journey to the hide-out.

Abbie therefore resolved to lay an ambush and try and take them alive and extract information regarding the location of the raiders' den, and with this plan in mind she was constantly seeking to find a suitable place for staging a hold-up.

Finally, she found a location that she thought would serve their purpose. The southern trail entered a shallow valley that contained a number of deep depressions, one of which could well conceal the presence of the posse. Unfortunately this hollow lay at least 200 yards from the trail and she would need someone much closer to halt the drivers. After some little thought, Abbie decided that she herself would have to be the one to initially bring the Comancheros to a halt.

Over the protests of her companions, she spelt out the details of her plan. One of the Ute braves would hide to the north of the ambush location and would signal when the carts came into view. The posse would conceal themselves in the selected hollow ready to come storming up when Abbie fired a shot from her pistol. Meanwhile, she would stand by the track, apparently unarmed. The perfect figure of a young damsel in distress, with her horse lying on the ground obviously spent and looking as though he was in a dying condition.

Since she wanted a situation where the suspicions of the Comancheros would be completely lulled, Abbie stressed that there was to be no smoking, since the odour of tobacco smoke wafting on the slightest breeze could put her plan in jeopardy. The tracks of the posse where they had joined up with the southern trail were carefully brushed out. The posse took up their positions in the hollow and Abbie waited by the trail, ready to pull her bay down onto his side with the whispered command to 'lie down'.

All was ready and the waiting was the most anxious time. Abbie slid her gun-belt around so that her pinfire revolver was hidden by her left hip and by her riding coat. She unlaced the thong securing the front of her buckskin shirt to reveal the tops of her breasts and rubbed some dirt on her face to create a dishevelled appearance. Then she sat down by her horse and waited.

The time passed slowly, and it was with extreme relief that Abbie heard the twitter of a sand bird, or rather a perfect imitation rendered by her Ute scout. Abbie rose and got her bay lying down. She looked around. Nothing could be seen of the party in the hollow but to the north she could observe first of all dust and then the outline of the expected carts. Now she had to play out her role.

Abbie removed her hat and began to wave it excitedly to attract the full attention of the oncoming Comancheros. Simultaneously she began to cry out, 'Por favor, Señores!' giving every appearance of a young girl relieved because no doubt these kind men would assist her in her obvious predicament. As they came much closer, she was a trifle concerned to note that each cart had two men, a driver and a companion who was probably a guard to assist in the event of a hold-up. Mentally, Abbie shrugged her shoulders. She couldn't change her plan at this late date.

The two carts came close and halted the patient oxen, no doubt glad of the rest. The four men stared down at her as Abbie, acting out her role, clasped her hands with apparent joy and thanked the kind men who had arrived in time to save her from the desert.

They looked at her and looked at each other, more than one with an evil grin on his ugly dirty visage.

Finally, one with stained yellow teeth and a livid scar extending from his right eye across his cheek, exclaimed, 'Well! Who's going to be the first to take her? If you men are shy, I'll be the one to give her a taste of love from a real man!' And he rose in preparation to descend from the cart.

Abbie turned away as though in fright, drew her

pistol and swung back moving the gun back and forth to cover the four men. 'Not today, *chico*! Just get your hands up in the air, all of you!'

Scarface made the mistake of moving towards her and Abbie placed a shot an inch above his belt buckle. Knowing the nature of the men on the carts and fully aware of the grim work in which they were engaged, she had no compunction in delivering what would undoubtedly be a mortal wound. He clasped his stomach and screamed in agony as he stared down at the blood rapidly covering his grubby hands.

Momentarily frozen by the effect of her one shot, Abbie looked at the anguished features of her victim and for a brief moment took her eyes off the other three Mexicans. She was brought back to reality as she heard the snick-snick of a shotgun's ears being hammered back and the piece being swung in her direction. Frantically, Abbie threw herself down and rolled to the right so that she was hidden from view by the oxen.

She vanished as the shotgun roared. Both loads of buckshot cut the air where Abbie had been standing micro-seconds before and she rose from where she had rolled in time to see the shot-gunner frantically attempting to recharge his muzzle-loading weapon. There was no hesitation on Abbie's part. Her pinfire had remained locked in her two-handed grip as she had performed the movements to save her life and she rapidly triggered two shots at her adversary. He stopped suddenly in his reloading operations and, as though tired, slumped sideways and fell to the ground.

Meanwhile, during the shooting the two drivers had sat open mouthed with their hands high in the air.

At the sound of the shots, the remainder of the posse came boiling up out of the hollow where they had been concealed. They surrounded the carts, whooping and congratulating Abbie on the success of her plan. Meanwhile, the two drivers, visibly shaking, sat very still with their hands above their sombreros as their compatriot's agonies were reduced to a steady whimper as he quietly expired.

Abbie called for Felipe. 'Now, Felipe! This is where we will be relying upon your skills of interrogation. I want to know where the raiders' camp is located. About how many men are there? How many guards surround the camp and where they are located? Furthermore find out if there is any kind of password needed to enter the camp?'

As Felipe turned, she grasped his arm, 'Felipe, you might add that if they attempt to lie to me or anything they say turns out to be false we will turn them over to the Indians – actually to Minny, who would just love to decorate their skins with that razor-sharp Bowie that she carries!'

Hearing her name mentioned. Minny came forward and; recognizing the word 'Bowie', drew the knife and flourished it menacingly to the now terrified Mexican drivers.

Felipe spoke to them in the most severe manner he could muster, stating the information that he wanted to extract by listing them point by point on his fingers and periodically pointing to Minny and her ever-constant

Bowie knife. They responded excitedly, evidently telling him all that he wanted to know, clasping their hands together and periodically making the sign of the cross to emphasize that every word that they uttered was the truth. No doubt they were also praying that they would not be turned over to the terrible squaw who stood there brandishing her wicked-looking knife with an evil grin upon her face.

At length Felipe turned to Abbie and produced an accurate picture of all that he had obtained from the two petrified drivers. 'Señorita Abbie, these men tell me that it is a three-day journey for them from the hacienda to the gang's location close to the border. They could not tell me in miles, but only in the time needed to drive a team of oxen there.

'There are usually about twenty men in the camp and they have at least two on guard, one facing the northern trail and the other facing the Rio Grande, which is in sight to the south.

'They tell me that when they recognize certain landmarks they leave the main trail south and travel for about half an afternoon until they reach the camp. I'm sorry, Abbie. I could not obtain more details but neither has a watch or clock so they have to determine the time by the sun and when they get hungry. I tried to get details so we could draw a sketch map but these are two very ignorant peons. They did not understand what I meant about a map.'

Abbie smiled at the rather crestfallen boy and assured him, 'Never mind, Felipe! I think that you've done very well.'

She called for two lengths of line and had a noose fashioned in each piece. The two drivers stared and shook their heads in horror, believing that they were to be hanged. Abbie, through Felipe, quietened their fears and instructed them to don the nooses with the knots at the back of their necks. They were then to slide the ropes down their backs inside their shirts and two of the Rangers tied the free end to the body of their respective cart. Thus haltered, they were safe as long as they sat in their driver's seat. But any excessive movement and they would strangle themselves.

'Now, *amigos*, I want you to drive the carts just the way you always have. I'll give you further instructions when we get nearer to the end of our journey. To make sure that you keep your minds on the job,' Abbie paused and indicated Minny, 'This Ute *señorita* will be in charge of both of you and will make sure that you play no tricks! Do you understand?'

Felipe gave a graphic translation of what Abbie had said and glumly the two drivers swore by all the saints that they would do their very best to comply with all the Señorita Minny's instructions.

Abbie gave instructions that the two deceased guards were to be buried off the trail in a little arroyo.

'There's to be no grave markers. It is not nice, but it's important that nobody coming south should see anything out of the ordinary. Perhaps when we are coming north again we can then mark the spot.'

With one of the two Ute braves ranging ahead and scouting the countryside, the posse headed south, their speed limited by the lumbering ox-drawn wagons. Due to the latter, the time tended to pass slowly which gave Abbie time to consider and reject various plans of assault on the raiders' hide-out. At length she formulated a scheme that, with good timing, stood a reasonable chance of success.

On the last evening before the day when the carts would normally arrive at the camp Abbie called the men together – except for the two prisoners still watched over by the ever-vigilant Minny.

With all the men listening attentively, Abbie outlined her plan to attack the raiders in their hide-out.

'Now, as you know, the enemy will be expecting the ox carts laden with supplies that they cannot get by raiding or foraging. Now I don't know how many of you are familiar with the story of the Trojan War but those two carts are going to be our Trojan Horse.'

Most of the men looked puzzled, so Abbie gave them a brief outline of the famed story, explaining how the Greeks captured Troy by means of the men hidden inside the horse. 'We are going to have four men, two to each cart, hidden under those canvas tarps and ready to emerge shooting when inside the camp.'

One of the Rangers interjected, 'What about the northern lookout? He'll be able to look down into those carts and could easily see that something is wrong!'

'Good point, Joe! One of our Ute braves will have to locate that lookout and silence him before the carts reach his position. Then he'll have to assume his role and signal the camp that the carts are coming. I gather from the drivers that there is no sort of code, just a shout from up in the rocks. Our man should also contact us, using a mirror, when the carts have successfully passed the lookout position, and that will be the signal for the main party to move in close ready to storm in directly the shooting starts. Any questions?'

The men of the posse looked at each other and finally one asked, 'Who are the four men who're to be this here Trojan horse?'

'Well Jake, I think that I'll let you men decide that among yourselves. I personally think that the ones selected should be young and agile, and really good shots with both revolvers and long guns.'

And, adding a little bit of flattery, she added. 'That's the trouble, you're all experts as far as I'm concerned. That's why you'll have to decide amongst yourselves. Draw cards if necessary.' And Abbie turned away to allow the posse to decide who should be the four men.

The posse gathered around with the men speaking animatedly as they discussed the choices for the 'Trojan Horse' party. Finally, they called to Abbie and nominated their choices.

George Lawson, the remaining ranch hand from Abbie's ranch, whose brother had headed north to raise more men, was the posse's first choice. He was joined by three Rangers: Tom Budner, Bill Wilson and Red O'Hara, the last being an outwardly shy lad of nineteen who Abbie was assured was the fastest gun of them all.

The posse rode on and eventually, on the afternoon of the third day, turned off the main trail and made their way over a barely discernible track toward the raiders' lair.

The accident happened quite suddenly. As Bill Wilson's horse was picking its way daintily among the rock-strewn trail, it disturbed a solitary rattlesnake taking advantage to sun itself on a warm slab of stone. The horse's hoof landed close to the reptile and it reared its head, hissing angrily with its little forked tongue flickering back and forth. Bill's horse was startled by the snake and leapt sideways in fear, with the unfortunate rider being thrown from the saddle. Several of the posse members chuckled at Bill's mishap and then fell silent as he rose to his feet clutching his right arm and grimacing with pain.

'Dammit! I've got a busted wing! What the hell are we gonna do now?' Bill's medical analysis of the result of his accident was only too evident as he stood there with his right arm bent at a most abnormal angle.

His arm was splinted and put in a sling made from his polka dot bandanna. Abbie looked down at him quizzically, 'Well Bill it would seem that you have withdrawn from the Trojan horse party rather suddenly.'

She smiled at the crestfallen Ranger to take the sting out of her remark. 'Now we need somebody to take your place and I'm nominating that the fourth person will be me! No arguments, gentlemen,' as a chorus of protests broke out. 'My mind is made up so let's just get ready for this attack!'

CHAPTER FIFTEEN

Abbie lay uncomfortably on the rough-hewn boards that formed the bed of the Comancheros' cart that was conveying her closer to the outlaw hide-out every minute. Hidden under the canvas tarpaulin that concealed both her and George Lawson, the late afternoon sun beating down upon their canvas roof created an oven where the heat underneath was unpleasantly oppressive, causing both of them to be constantly bathed in perspiration.

It was no consolation to know that the occupants of the other cart were undergoing the same unpleasant experience. Adding to their ordeal was the fact that both carts had been used to convey the clothing of the slain victims and the boards, having been soaked with blood, attracted all the flies in Texas.

The flies, the odour, the overpowering heat, the thumps and jolts as the cumbersome cart lurched its way onward, coupled with the constant screech of one axle desperately in need of lubrication, made each of the four long for the journey to end.

Apart from a few whispered comments, each of the four endured their purgatory in silence. They all awaited with eager anticipation the distinctive repeated cry of the desert red-tailed hawk uttered by the Ute brave that would indicate that the northern sentry had been put out of commission and that he had taken his place.

At long last the cry came. Abbie drew her Pinfire pistol and whispered to Lawson, 'Get ready, George!'

To their Mexican driver she said with a significant jerk at his noose, 'Now, Pablo, no tricks! Stop the cart in the usual place and just sit still! We'll do the rest.'

By doing a contortionist act and squinting, she was just able to peer forward and see between the fat legs of Pablo and the rear ends of their two oxen. There was little to see at first and then glimpses of roughly built structures as the two carts arrived at their destination. Pablo called out a polite greeting of '*Buenos días, señores,*' which was answered by a curt inaudible reply. The cart was brought to a halt and Abbie threw back the tarpaulin.

For a split second she was blinded by the sudden glare of the western sun and as she rose to her feet the trio of Mexicans standing close to the cart reacted violently to her sudden appearance. One reached for the pistol nestled in his sash, while the other two reached behind them for the long guns propped against a hitching rail. Abbie triggered two snap shots at the *pistolero* and dived over the far side of the cart where, kneeling, she fired another two rounds at the riflemen. Meanwhile, George Lawson had swiftly followed her example and also fired at the Mexicans before joining her and firing under the cart. With a loud wail their driver fell backwards into the bed of his cart, where he tried to flatten himself against the boards.

By this time the other Rangers had emerged from their cart and were busy engaging still more of the raiders, who spilled out of the weathered shacks for all the world like outraged wasps responding to an upturned hive. Fortunately, many had appeared drawn by the noise but were not immediately prepared to tackle an enemy since most of their assortment of guns had to be loaded and primed. They dropped back into doorways and behind walls to ready their pieces.

A thunder of hoofs heralded the arrival of the rest of the posse, who quickly threw themselves from their horses and delivered independent fire at any unfortunate outlaw who allowed himself to be seen.

Felipe, following earlier instructions, called upon the raiders to throw out their guns and come out with hands held high above their heads. Fully half of the Mexicans started to comply with the order, which was delivered repeatedly in Spanish. Guns clattered onto the ground in front of the track but as they arose to surrender a harsh voice, cursing continually, ordered them to fight on.

The fighting for control of the outlaws' hide-out became a confusing medley of shots, shouting, screams, and cries of pain as lead bullets found their marks, and curses all overlaid by an increasingly thick cloud of grey smoke pungent with the odour of bad eggs.

Abbie and George, working as a team, quickly determined that the three Mexicans who had reacted violently to their presence were no longer a problem and moved quickly to reload their revolvers. For Abbie, this was a simple matter of punching the empty shells from the cylinder of her pistol and reloading from her pouch. George carried a spare primed cylinder for his .36 calibre Navy Colt but he had to knock out the barrel wedge, disassemble the pistol, remove the fired cylinder and replace it with another from his jacket pocket before he was ready for action once more.

Abbie waited patiently. When George nodded that he was ready, they rolled under the cart and dived for the doorway of a shack, in front of which lay the three dead Mexicans. The shack was empty. They then commenced a shack-clearing operation, moving from building to building on their side of the track, winkling out and shooting or disarming any outlaws they encountered in their progress. The pair were joined by the erstwhile occupants of the other Comancheros' cart and the deadly quartet made short work of the opposition.

Cries from across the dusty track indicated that the posse members on that side were having equal success and a blocking force of three men who had ridden right through the hide-out thwarted any attempts of outlaws to break out towards the Rio Grande. At length the shooting and the noise died down and there was relative silence. Abbie's men began to emerge from their firing positions when there was a roar of defiance and a blood-stained figure rose from behind a water trough. He began screaming in Spanish his hatred of all gringos as he started shooting wildly to where Abbie was standing amid a knot of her men. His first shot thudded into a post of the building behind them, his second brought a curse from George Lawson as he buckled at the knees and the next moment the outlaw fell backwards, lifeless with two of Abbie's 12mm bullets in his head.

Now was the time to collect the prisoners and count the cost. A full dozen of the raiders had surrendered and were sitting disarmed with their hands on their heads. A thorough search of the hide-out discovered fifteen dead outlaws for a cost of one dead Ranger and four men wounded, including George Lawson. None of their wounds was sufficiently serious that they would be unable to ride.

The wounded of both sides were treated and the dead buried. The lone fallen Ranger was given a grave on a slight rise to the east of the outlaw hide-out and the spot marked with a cross, while the unknown dead raiders were buried in a mass grave excavated by some of their former comrades under the watchful eyes of armed guards. One building was found crammed with booty stolen from Mexicans south of the border. There was simply no way of determining the ownership of these pathetic articles and so Abbie reluctantly ordered that the building be dowsed with cooking oil found in a make-shift kitchen. The storeroom was to be set on fire when the posse commenced their trek north the following day.

That evening after the short but sharp battle to

secure the outlaws' hide-out, Abbie sat sipping a welcome cup of coffee. Rather than a sense of elation at the success of her mission, a reaction had set in, and she was in a sombre mood as she reviewed the many steps in her life that had brought her to this present position, starting with the infidelity of her late husband Bertie Penraven, and how the role of gun-fighter and leader had been gradually thrust upon her. Were these qualities actually thrust, she reflected, or did she seek them out?

The gunplay that had marked the later stages of her life in the west had in the main allowed her no choice; it was kill or be killed, and Abbie had never had a desire to die. The way that she automatically assumed a leadership role was more curious. Living as she did in an era where women were automatically expected to be subservient to men, it was certainly strange how the vast majority of them willingly permitted her to take command. Was it because she had a military childhood in an environment where people of her caste just gave orders and in the main they were promptly carried out, or was it something deeper? Was there something within her that prompted her to challenge the mores of the society into which she had been born?

Abbie mentally shrugged her shoulders. There were simply no answers to her self-analysis. She knew in her heart that her father would have been proud of her achievements, though possibly a trifle dubious of the gunfighting reputation of his little daughter.

That brought her to thinking about another aspect

of her life. Was there any room for romance and marriage in her life? Although she knew that she had all the healthy yearnings of a young female, Abbie smiled a trifle wryly at the thought of any man who would care to enter into a relationship with a gun-slinging *pistolera*. On the other hand, she did not want to live out her existence as an old maid.

Unable to find solutions to any of the things she pondered over, Abbie wrapped herself in her blanket and drifted into a shallow sleep.

The following morning plans were made to return to the ranger camp at Trinidad. The discovery of a large quantity of leg irons in one of the huts solved the problem of how to restrain the prisoners. Each was securely shackled and conveyed northward, six to a cart, with the posse members spread out on either side. In vain, the prisoners complained that they were cramped, that there was no room for them to sit. Abbie was remorseless and had Felipe remind them that the alternative was to be shot on the spot. That would solve the problem for everyone! After that suggestion there was silence.

The buildings were torched and the column headed north with the ox carts. The journey was slow and tedious, governed by the speed of the plodding oxen, and the last leg was a night march so that prying eyes were less likely to report their arrival at the Ranger camp to the hacienda.

Captain McHugh was elated by the success of the mission and was eager to hear Abbie's report as soon as she had dismissed the posse after having seen to the prisoners and cared for the livestock. She rendered a detailed description of their journey and the attack, emphasizing the roles played by various members and not forgetting the supreme sacrifice made by Bert Thompson, the dead Ranger.

As they spent the evening reviewing the situation, there was an unexpected but pleasant interruption as the reinforcements guided by Fred Lawson arrived at the camp. Such was Abbie's reputation in and around Colorado City that Jack Harding had had no difficulty in raising a further column of hard-bitten riders. In addition, there were several more Ute braves and, of course, Wilf Bateson and his team of five gunners and their cherished two-pounder. The newcomers were made very welcome and did not take long to settle in as they went around greeting men they already knew and in turn being introduced to the original real Texas Rangers.

Meanwhile, Abbie and David McHugh continued with their review of the outlaw situation. McHugh described how he had more or less placed the outlaw hacienda under an interdict. That is, by using a continual screen of riders, he had prevented anyone from Trinidad going out to the hacienda and therefore revealing any information regarding the Ranger camp or their activities. Due to the limited number of riders, it had been a wearying time but with the reinforcements from the north the task should be easier.

The second thing he had done was to have the hacienda under perpetual observation, noting any coming or going of the inhabitants. Once a party of Indians, identified as Comanche by their appearance, had visited the ranch and when leaving they had been accompanied by more than a dozen riders, Mexicans or Americanos, together with a train of pack mules. McHugh surmised that the contents of the mule packs were probably some of the looted material from the raids south of the border.

'Now here's a curious thing, Abbie! Among the riders from the fort was a man dressed differently. I tried to get Lone Wolf the scout to describe his apparel to me but we lacked common words. Well I was reading a book of Sir Walter Scott – Ivanhoe – that I'd picked up several weeks ago and hadn't had time to read until recently. The book was illustrated and was open when Lone Wolf made his report. He looked down at the picture in the book and his eyes literally bulged. He pointed to the knight and the breastplate he was wearing, pointed in the direction of the Hacienda and back at the picture, saying "hombre, hombre!", telling me that one of the outlaws was wearing armour!'

Abbie interrupted him excitedly, 'Last year we encountered "Old Iron Shirt" and his band of Comanche just south of Colorado City. In fact, Jack Harding, my foreman, took a long-distance shot at him and hit him in the shoulder. Could he be leading a band around here?'

Captain McHugh shook his head, 'No, Abbie! That Iron Shirt got his comeuppance in the May of this year when he and his men were in a fight with Rangers and settlers. He was most undoubtedly killed and the shirt, which was chain mail, not a breastplate, was broken up and divided among the men as a souvenir of the fight. This fella, we'll call Young Iron Shirt, was most definitely a white man posing as an Indian, probably pretending to be the reincarnation of the dead Comanche. Most of the braves, being superstitious, would be in awe of such a person. Meanwhile, what's our next move? Or rather, pardner, what's your next move, since this bullet wound, though healing, still won't permit me to ride.'

'Let me have a few moments to get my thoughts in order and I may be able to propose a possible scheme.' She fell silent, her head bowed forward with her sun-bleached hair glinting in the light from the campfire.

McHugh watched her silently, trying to suppress the affectionate feeling that he was beginning to feel for this English girl. He knew that he was fond of her and was overjoyed when she had returned from the expedition to the south. On the other hand, he was mindful of his wife and two small children that he had left behind in the cabin on the banks of the Brazos River and the vows that he had made. His thoughts were interrupted when the subject of his thoughts raised her head.

Abbie had already given their next phase of the operation considerable thought and she succinctly outlined what she thought would be the best plan of attack.

'I think that the best plan would be to attack Young Iron Shirt when he and his followers are out in the open. If they are behind the walls of the hacienda and we have to storm the premises we are likely to take unacceptable casualties, which I for one do not want. How long was Young Iron Shirt away on his last foray?'

McHugh consulted a page in his notebook. 'Our scout told me that the sun rose and set five times before he returned to the hacienda. I would suspect that his next trading expedition would be shortly.'

'Right, so if we can silently gain control of his head-quarters while he is away visiting his Comanche customers we can present him with quite a problem upon his return, especially if we have half our force available to surround him from the desert side. He'll be pinned between two fires, the walls of his own hacienda manned by our men and the guns of our mobile force.'

In general terms Captain McHugh indicated that Abbie's plan was sound. 'But,' he cautioned. 'Do we have enough men to mount such an operation?'

They both pondered the issue of manpower, coming to the conclusion that with Abbie's original posse, the Texas Ranger patrol, the new posse members from Colorado City and the Utes – not forgetting the gunners of Wilf Bateson's detachment – they could muster close on fifty fighters minus a prison guard and someone to assist the wounded men remaining in camp.

They decided that the walking wounded such as McHugh himself and George Lawson, together with young Jed Oldberg and one Ranger, would be enough to guard both the leg-shackled prisoners and the camp. When the last three mentioned were called and instructed on their role in the coming operation there were immediate protests at being left behind, especially on the part of young Jed who was anxious to prove himself in Abbie's eyes. A little flattery on her part soon mollified the boy and he puffed with pride at being compared to the Texas Rangers.

The next thing was to receive swift information directly Young Iron Shirt and his riders left the hacienda together with Indians and the mule train. To this end, another scout was sent out to locate the one keeping the hacienda under observation with orders to report as soon as Iron Shirt left once more. Meanwhile, the assault force was ordered to be ready to move at a moment's notice.

There was one thing more to be done. Abbie, after consultation with Captain McHugh, sent Felipe into La Trinidad to quietly enquire if there was a Mexican musician in town who was accomplished on a bugle or trumpet. If such a person existed he was to bring him back to the camp.

'OK, Abbie! Perhaps you'd better spell out in more detail the operation by means of which you are intending to gain control of the hacienda!'

'Well it would be nice if we could capture the buildings without suffering any casualties, but I don't know whether that is possible. This is what I'm proposing. We take our force by night and create a cordon right around the hacienda with the men just out of sight. We position Wilf Bateson and his cannon aimed at the southern wall.

'Just as the sun is rising, Wilf will send one shot slamming into the adobe of that southern wall and then he and his men quickly move their piece to a new position just out of rifle range facing the main gate on the east side. At the same time, the cordon moves in closer with the men continually shifting around to make it difficult for defenders to determine the size of the attacking force. Felipe and I will ride forward and call upon the defenders of the hacienda to surrender. I will tell them that if they lay down their arms they will be treated decently. However, if they resist then the order will be "no quarter" and all will be put to the sword.

'Felipe will give a signal to the group standing by the gun and at that moment our trumpeter will start playing "The Deguello". I'm told that every Mexican knows the story of the battle of the Alamo and how that piece of music was used to signal that there were to be no survivors. I would inform the leader of the defenders that if they had not surrendered by the time our musician ends "The Deguello" then the consequences will indeed be dire for him and his men. I just hope that Felipe can unearth a bugler or trumpeter.

'David, I know it is a big bluff and they may not fall for our tricks but it's worth a try. And I'm sorry having to use a reference to an incident which is almost sacred to all Texans but we have to put absolute fear into those men in the hacienda.'

David McHugh looked at Abbie in awe and more than a sense of bewilderment, 'Abbie Penraven! I always was led to believe that young ladies raised in your Victoria's England were genteel creatures but you

136

have the mind of an Apache horse thief! Where on earth do you get these notions from?'

'Well! You forget that I was raised in India as the daughter of a serving officer. My father always permitted me to be present when he was entertaining his fellows and so I sat demurely and soaked up all sorts of military information not normally available to the average girl or boy for that matter!

'Anyway, I'm not important! Let's just get this operation under way!'

Shortly before they and the rest of the camp sought their blankets, Felipe turned up. In tow he had a small frightened fellow countryman clutching a tarnished brass trumpet.

'Señorita, I heard this man playing in one of the saloons and so when he left I politely asked him if he would accompany me to the Ranger camp. He assures me that he can play any piece of Mexican music ever written and he volunteers to work for the Rangers. Don't you, Tomasio?'

As he said this last remark Felipe raised the Navy Colt that was hidden down his right leg and waved it suggestively at his companion, who stared back, giving the appearance of a small rabbit confronted by a fox.

Abbie realized that Felipe had used the old Royal Navy method of obtaining volunteers and had press-ganged Tomasio at the point of a gun. Quickly, she smiled at their musician and, patting him reassuringly on the shoulder, indicated that he would be well paid for his little performance.

CHAPTER SIXTEEN

Time dragged as they waited for a report from one of the scouts and finally in the late morning of the fourth day one of the Ute braves appeared and described how a band of Comanche, together with Young Iron Shirt, ten of his men and a full dozen heavily laden mules had headed north into the Staked Plain.

Captain McHugh called to Sergeant Campbell, 'Sergeant, organize a last hot meal and get the men ready for a night march.'

The sergeant saluted and hurried away to comply with the orders which, of course, included all men present as the newcomers had earlier taken the oath as temporary Texas Rangers. As darkness fell over the land, the column moved out, twenty men in the vanguard followed by the artillery piece and then the remainder of the force. The order was 'no talking' and both Abbie and Sergeant Campbell rode up and down the column enforcing the command.

First light found them encircling the hacienda, a chain of silent mounted statues just beyond the estimated distance of rifle range. To the south stood Wilf Bateson, a lighted linstock shielded but ready to be thrust into the primed touch hole of the gun whose barrel was aimed squarely at the adobe wall, a dark mass against the lighter desert background. His men knelt around their piece ready to serve it with additional powder and explosive shells if required.

Abbie was mounted on her faithful bay facing the closed main gate of the hacienda and accompanied by Felipe. Behind her, as a single link of that encircling chain, was their now not merely reluctant but openly terrified musician, who was being encouraged to perform his duty by the Bowie-wielding Minny.

It grew lighter and finally the sun peeped its head over the eastern horizon. Abbie raised a white handkerchief as a signal that could just be seen by the waiting gunners. When her hand dropped, Wilf lowered the glowing linstock to the waiting touchhole. The priming quill spluttered and then the piece spoke, bellowing out its message across the empty plains. At that relatively short range the boom of the gun was followed simultaneously by the crash as the shell smashed into the adobe and exploded.

The result was far more devastating than any of the attacking force had expected as when the smoke and adobe dust settled it could be seen that a vee-shaped hole reaching from the point of impact to the very top had been ripped out of the wall.

'Load!' ordered Bateson and his gun team ran through their oft-rehearsed drill of swabbing out and reloading their beloved gun with powder, wad and shot. As they completed, Wilf's arm shot in the air, signalling to Abbie that their piece was ready to fire once more. At that signal Abbie rode forward with Felipe holding a white flag of truce on the end of his rifle. She drew her pistol, fired two shots in the air and waited.

From beyond the walls could be heard loud cries and curses in Spanish intermingled with voices speaking in English. Eventually a series of heads appeared peering over the walls of the hacienda and one close to the main gate cried out, 'What you want?'

Abbie rode forward several paces, accompanied by Felipe. 'My name is Commandante Penraven of the Texas Rangers and I am ordering you to surrender this hacienda. There is no escape. As you can see I have at hand 100 men surrounding you and artillery with which to smash your defences. You are to open the main gate and come out with your hands high in the air and line up against the front wall.'

As Abbie slowly and distinctly issued her instructions, Felipe translated them into Spanish so that there could be no mistakes or confusion as to her message.

She continued: 'Those are my orders. If you chose to ignore them my bugler will play a little tune to help you make up your minds. I'm sure that most of you are familiar with "The Deguello" and you know what it implies.

'If my bugler comes to the end of his music and there is no surrender we will immediately attack and there will be no quarter given. You have the choice, surrender or die!' And Abbie turned and nodded to Tomasio who, encouraged by a gentle prod of Minny's Bowie knife, began a wavering version of the music, which however got louder and stronger as he continued.

Heads popped up and down as the defenders discussed their limited choices and finally, just before the tune commenced its finale and Abbie had begun to think that her ploy had failed, the gates ahead of her and Felipe swung open and a number of dejected men came forth, accompanied to their surprise by four women, who alternatively wept and screamed defiance in regard to their new circumstances.

As they lined up with hands high, Abbie rode up close and addressed the one who had spoken from the wall. 'Have you brought out everyone? No tricks now! I demand the truth!'

The one she addressed, a short squat individual with long greasy hair and drooping mustachios, was eager to make himself agreeable to the new regime. '*Sí Señora Commandante*, we all agreed that we would surrender. That is except for one foolish man who insisted we should wait for *el Jefe* to return.

'My knife settled the little dispute. He is lying in the courtyard.' He smiled ingratiatingly up at Abbie.

She had taken an instant aversion to the creature in front of her and had mentally renamed him 'Slimy'! She therefore ignored him and waved Sergeant

Campbell forward. He detailed half a dozen men to
take charge of the prisoners and began to move them
back towards La Trinidad, where they would join the
earlier captives resulting from the raid on the outlaw
camp.

'Not you, Slimy!' stated Abbie as she separated him
from the rest of the prisoners 'Felipe! Tell him he is to
remain and escort us through the hacienda.'

When Felipe translated this information to the
greasy little Mexican he, rather than being honoured
for being singled out, protested vehemently that his
place was with his fellow captives and Abbie wondered
why as she stifled his whining with a single '*Silencio*!'

The rest of the column had moved in together with
Wilf Bateson and his gunners after they disarmed their
cannon and, as the prisoners were heading east over
the hills, they all entered the courtyard of the mysteri-
ous hacienda.

All was still apart from a couple of buzzards that rose
aloft from where they had just started a meal off the
fellow that Slimy had knifed. Abbie and Felipe dismounted and tied their horses to the hitching rail in
front of the covered porch that ran around three sides
of the courtyard. Then, while the remainder of the
column attended to their mounts and stood at ease
with drawn pistols, they motioned Slimy to commence
his tour of the premises.

Although the buildings still showed signs of the fire
that had ravaged the place as a result of the long past
Comanche raid, Abbie was impressed with the renova-
tions that had been made. The trio walked on shining

tiled floors past painted walls hung with coloured blankets and adorned with native art work.

Slimy, eager to prove his acceptance of the new
order of things, showed them store rooms bulging with
stolen goods and others with ample foodstuffs with
which to feed the garrison. Then he escorted them
through the private quarters of Young Iron Shirt and
Abbie was intrigued to note that the leader spared
nothing to make his life one of luxury.

In a passageway leading back to the courtyard she
noticed a flight of steps leading down into the darkness. 'What's down there?' she demanded.

Slimy ignored her question and motioned for her
and Felipe to come and examine the stables. Felipe
grabbed him by the shoulder. 'Not so fast, *amigo*!
The Commandante asked you a question.' He lit a
candle resting in a nearby wall sconce and with light
in one hand and his pistol in the other he, none too
gently, pushed the outlaw down the steps ahead of
them.

The air grew colder as the trio descended and after
twenty steps were brought up short by a stout iron-
studded door. Their reluctant guide shrugged his
shoulders and said 'See it is nothing. Just old things
stored down here. I did not want to bother you,
Commandante!'

Abbie had thought that she heard sounds as they
came down the steps and motioned for him to be
quiet.

There were noises coming from beyond the door,
although she could not identify them. Suddenly she

stuck her pistol deep into his stomach, so that he gasped with the pain and demanded, 'Where is the key to that door? Quickly now before I lose patience with you!'

Felipe translated her words to the trembling outlaw and slowly he drew a large key from his right pocket. He inserted the key into a large well-oiled lock and opened the door. When he did so there came forth a stench that made both Abbie and Felipe gag. The latter held the candle high and peered into an underground chamber. What they saw was like a scene from Dante's vision of Hell. The room was crowded with filthy dirty emaciated beings, human by their shape but shackled at the ankles to stout rings set in the walls and from the sounds that arose gave an appearance of savage animals.

At the sight of Slimy they all cowed back with hands raised to their faces in abject terror. 'Who are these poor creatures and why are they so scared of you?'

Slimy did not answer, just smiled his greasy smile and shrugged his shoulders: '*Quién sabe*!'

'Felipe, tell these people that they are to be freed!' Felipe explained who he and the lady *pistolera* were and when he finally silenced the shrieks of almost insane rejoicing he demanded to know why they were all incarcerated.

One old man with a grey beard below his waist became their spokesman. He was a builder and had been hired to renovate the burnt-out hacienda. Most of the fellow captives were his workmen. When they had completed their work they had been imprisoned here. The others were men who had strayed too close to the area and had been grabbed by the guards. Normally they were driven up to do menial work, under armed guard, inside the walls of the hacienda but nobody had come near for two whole days and some of the men were desperate for food and water. There was a key on the wall with which to unlock the shackles but it was out of their reach where it hung alongside a vicious-looking bullwhip.

Noticing Slimy sinking back into the background, Abbie roughly called him forward to unlock the captives. Hesitantly, he came forward and did as he was told. No sooner had he released the first batch than they leapt upon him and, ignoring Abbie's cries of 'stop' and even a bullet fired into the ceiling, they proceeded to beat him savagely with their chains and finally to garrotte him, only ceasing when he slumped lifeless on the stone floor of the cell.

The ex-builder turned apologetically to Abbie. 'I'm sorry, *señorita*, but that man was a devil. Every day when he entered the cell he beat us with that whip you see hanging on the wall. He would deliberately aim for the faces and one or two of us lost an eye for his pleasure. We all swore that if ever we had the chance we kill him we would. Not for vengeance, you understand, but for the sake of justice!'

Abbie nodded. There was little she could say. Although she was horrified by the way they had meted out justice, she knew that one could not apply civilized standards in such a situation. Turning to Felipe, she instructed him to see that the freed prisoners were taken up to the well-stocked kitchen and fed. They were to remain there while the Rangers completed the second part of their operation, namely the capture of Young Iron Shirt.

CHAPTER SEVENTEEN

While Abbie and Felipe had been on their tour of the hacienda, Sergeant Campbell and the other men of the column had been busy. The debris from the cannon shot had been cleared away and some convenient baulks of timber used both to brace the wall on either side where the shot had fallen but also to make a makeshift barricade across the gaping hole. Guards stood watch upon the walls and Abbie noted that they wore sombreros and serapes to give the appearance of the outlaws that they had replaced.

'Good work, Sergeant! Now maybe we can create a little surprise for Young Iron Shirt. Wilf! Would you and your gun team move the cannon into the shadows of the veranda and have it trained on the main gate. I suggest that you camouflage the outline somewhat so that it is not too obvious. Load the piece with a bag of that grapeshot that I saw among your supplies. That should do the trick if needed!'

Wilf Bateson nodded enthusiastically and he and his men manhandled their cannon onto a well-shaded corner as indicated and successfully hid its shape by moving some potted bushes in front to break up the angular shape of the piece.

Abbie stood in the centre of the courtyard and called for attention. 'Listen carefully, men. Sometime in the near future, Young Iron Shirt and his men are going to be returning. We don't know whether they will be alone or whether they may have Comanche guests with them. If possible I want this place to look as normal as possible. The men on the walls; if you're in view, cheer and wave at the chief upon his return. Those hidden below the parapet, restrain your curiosity until I give the word for you to rise and be seen. We want them to enter the courtyard and then we'll spring our surprise and we will try to get them to surrender. If they resist, shoot to kill!'

There were no questions as Abbie gave additional orders for food and drink to be distributed and suggested that those not on guard try to get some limited rest until ordered to stand to.

Having done all she could, Abbie returned to the well-appointed dining room, where she sank into a large armchair at the head of the table, sipping gratefully at a mug of coffee brought by Felipe. She thought over the dispositions of her little band. 'Have I covered every contingency? What if Young Iron Shirt spots the trap before entering the hacienda? How will he react? Will he attack or will he flee back into the *Llano Estacado*? How would my father have handled this situation?'

148

These thoughts and a thousand others flitted through her mind, and finally she permitted herself to fall into a sleep where Mexican bandits and Pathan tribesmen were plotting to attack a wagon train.

'*Señorita*! *Señorita*! Wake up! Riders are approaching!' Felipe shook Abbie respectfully but urgently, concerned that she would slip back into sleep.

Abbie shook her head to clear the cobwebs from her mind and, seeing a jug of water on the table, poured some onto her left hand and splashed it on her face. She hung her head, took a moment to collect her senses and then rose to her feet. Pausing only to draw her 12mm pinfire revolver and slip a sixth cartridge into the cylinder, Abbie holstered and, accompanied by Felipe, walked unhurriedly out of the building into the sunlit courtyard.

Squinting a little against the harsh brightness produced by the sun almost vertically overhead, Abbie climbed a ladder and peered cautiously over the parapet. There, off towards the north, was a swirling cloud of dust, in the midst of which could be seen the obscure figures of men and horses. In a very short time the vague outlines had developed into a group of mounted riders that grew rapidly larger and more distinct as the newcomers closed the distance between themselves and the hacienda.

Soon the majority of the riders could be identified by their headgear and clothing as Mexicans, among whom rode, in a fashion that suggested a familiarity of long standing, a group of bare-chested Indian braves. At the head of the riders astride a white mare was the lithe, youthful figure of a man wearing Indian garb but with his upper body encased in a breastplate of gleaming iron. His face was covered by a mask of black silk that successfully obscured his features and his long dark hair was secured by a red headband that held a single eagle feather.

A whispered order passed along the parapet prompted her men to wave their rifles in simulated joy at the return of 'their' leader and the large double gates were swung open wide for the entry of the riders.

Unsuspecting, they swept into the courtyard in a flurry of galloping hoofs and on a command from Young Iron Shirt they halted and threw themselves down from their sweating horses. Simultaneously, the gates closed and the Rangers turned inwards with their firearms pointed down at the newcomers.

Abbie drew her pistol and fired one shot in the air, causing all the dismounted riders to look up to where she was standing with her long-barreled revolver firmly held in both hands in her gunfighting mode as the muzzle moved slowly back and forth covering each man in turn.

'All of you men down there! Raise your hands in the air and freeze! You're covered by Texas Rangers and are all under arrest!'

Her words and the sight of the small female figure with her pistol outstretched towards them created a momentary frozen tableau as the outlaws digested her order and actions. Simultaneously, they all became aware that Abbie was not alone. The serape-draped figures all around the hacienda parapet had long guns and pistols pointing down into the courtyard, and they echoed her initial command with cries of 'Hands up!'

The frozen tableau exploded as all hell broke out among the riders bunched up in the courtyard. One or two reluctantly raised their hands in obedience to the summons but dropped them immediately in response to a shout from the iron-breasted figure of their leader. He screamed his defiance in Spanish and Comanche, while at the same time swinging down Indian fashion on the far side of his horse, drawing his pistol and firing it at Abbie from under the animal's neck. She felt the bullet pluck at her left arm as she dropped to one knee, reducing her outline against the sky and triggering a vain shot in reply while at the same time endeavouring to get a grasp on the general scene below her.

The Comanche warriors had turned as one and thrown themselves at the closed gate. One was success-ful in rising from his steed to grasp the top when a shotgun blast threw him to the ground. Most of the other outlaws dropped from the saddle and fired up at the Rangers on the walls above them, with predictable results since their horses were rearing and neighing in fright. The vast majority of their shot went completely wide of their targets, burrowing into and ricocheting off the walls, but at least one Ranger fell victim to the fusillade and fell from the catwalk.

The noise in the courtyard increased to a crescendo with the loud boom of Wilf Bateson's cannon fired at point-blank range into the mass of outlaws and their horses. The result of that one charge of grapeshot was ghastly as dozens of cast iron balls tore into humans and animals alike, reducing them to lifeless figures of blood-soaked flesh. The few outlaws still remaining on their feet raised their arms high pleading for mercy from the awful death-dealing cannon – all but one.

CHAPTER EIGHTEEN

Young Iron Shirt had been on the far side of the yard when the cannon fired and therefore the bodies of his men and their horses had provided cover for him and his white mare. Now, as his surviving men threw down their arms, he guided his horse to a position where he could drop to the ground and dart into the hacienda. Abbie slid down the ladder from the parapet and, pistol in hand, followed cautiously behind him, while in her wake came the ever faithful Felipe.

'Take care, *señorita*!' he whispered as they edged warily into the darkened hallway. 'The one we seek will be as vicious as an enraged bull!'

Abbie silently nodded her acceptance of his warning as she moved forward slowly, pressed against the wall with her pinfire grasped firmly in both hands.

An entry on her left led to the large dining room where she had rested before the arrival of the outlaws, and as she approached she heard a soft scuffling sound followed by a metallic clang. Peering carefully into the room lit only by the light given by two small windows high near the ceiling, she saw their quarry, having divested himself of his breastplate, was busy throwing on a ruffled shirt to match the concho-decorated pants that he had already donned over his bare legs. He created a bizarre figure as he stood by the massive oak table, giving an appearance of a Mexican grandee yet wearing a mask and still with a red headband adorned with a bedraggled feather.

A slight noise from Abbie prompted him to look in their direction. 'Ah!' he exclaimed, 'I see that we have unexpected guests. Welcome to the Hacienda Alvarez. I regret that my parents are not here to greet you but unfortunately they had to go away and I don't know when they will return!'

Abbie advanced further into the room and he apparently noticed for the first time that she was carrying a pistol. 'How dare you enter my house bearing arms? Do you not know who I am?' So saying he tore the black mask off and threw it on the floor, glaring at the two newcomers with both hands on his hips and with his chin raised imperiously towards them.

With Felipe on her left, Abbie stepped forward, covering Young Iron Shirt with her revolver as she answered the latter's question. 'You are, I believe, Antonio Alvarez, the only survivor of the Comanche raid on this hacienda, a raid that resulted in the deaths of your father, mother and younger sister!'

The dark-featured man before her twisted his face in a demonic grimace and his wild eyes glittered crazily. For the first time both she and Felipe noticed the blue-black markings on his chin, typical of the

154

tattoos of a Comanche warrior.

'Yes!' he boasted. 'I arranged that raid with my Comanche brothers. My dear parents said that I was sick and would have to go to a sanitorium for treatment but what they really wanted was to rob me of my inheritance and give it all to the little bitch who pretended to be my loving sister.

'It was so easy to arrange with the warriors who came to trade at our hacienda. The gates were left unlocked and the Comanche swept in. I thought that they would just take the things that they wanted and get rid of my unwanted family but no, they exceeded our agreement and looted and burned the place before carrying me off to be raised as a Comanche warrior. Many years passed before I could assert myself as one with authority among the people. Since then I have had the hacienda rebuilt and can pass with ease as either a Comanche chief, or if I desire pose as a Spanish *hidalgo*.'

Abbie stared at the crazed creature before her, horrified by his disclosures that he had arranged the murders of his parents and sister in order to satisfy his insane lust for wealth and power. 'You, *señor*, are no *hidalgo*! Rather you are a monster who has deliberately strayed far beyond the bounds of human decency. It is my duty therefore to arrest you so that you can answer for your crimes!'

Alvarez looked at her wildly and in a sudden movement produced a knife, which he threw underarm. Abbie was momentarily taken aback by the swiftness of his attack but Felipe responded faster by stepping in front of her. The knife had been thrown with deadly force and the Mexican lad sank to his knees with the weapon buried to the hilt in his stomach.

Even as Felipe dropped down clutching at the knife Abbie had drawn her pinfire pistol and, consumed with anger towards the evil heir of the hacienda, she triggered a shot, and again, and yet again, slamming each one into the centre of the white ruffled shirt worn by Antonio Alvarez. For a split second he stood there swaying, staring down at the crimson patch rapidly spreading across his shirt. There was a look of bewilderment fleeting across his face as if he was suddenly aware of his own mortality, and then he fell back lifeless into the massive chair that Abbie had occupied before the outlaws had appeared on the horizon.

Abbie knelt at Felipe's side, staring down at his pain-ravaged face. Gasping with the effort of speaking, he looked up and whispered, 'I'm sorry, *Commandante*! I had hoped to go back to my sister but it is not to be. Would you have the little priest of La Trinidad say a mass for me?'

With her eyes filled with tears and a strange lump in her throat, Abbie nodded her acceptance of the dying boy's request. She herself was not a particularly religious person and had been raised with a typical English upper class attitude towards things spiritual. There were things that one did in life such as going to church, being kind to animals, practising charity and so forth, but one did not dwell upon them. And so as Felipe grasped at her fingers with his bloody hands, Abbie searched for words that might comfort her dying companion. She finally said in a choking voice; '*Vayas con Dios, mi amigo*! Go with God, my friend.'

Felipe's hand loosened its grip and his head fell back. Abbie realized that she was alone in the room with two dead men, one, an enemy, the other a friend for whom she had developed a certain attachment over the weeks despite the vast difference in their cultural backgrounds.

Heavy footsteps broke in on her reverie and she looked up as Sergeant Campbell entered the room. He paused momentarily on the threshold at the tragic scene before him and then, as though to rouse Abbie from her sorrowful pose, in a loud voice rendered his report. 'It's all over, Cap'n Abbie! The last of the outlaws has surrendered but most of them shot it out to the end, as did the Comanche warriors. So we've only got three prisoners. Regretfully we lost two men from those on the walls, and, of course . . .' nodding towards Felipe's corpse . . . 'This poor lad here. Which, I might add, I'm sorry to see. What are your orders, Cap'n?'

Abbie rose to her feet and mentally shook herself with the realization that, regardless of her personal feelings, she was still in command of the expedition and decisions had to be made. She thought rapidly and assembled a series of suggestions of actions that should be taken.

'Well, Sergeant, this is what I think should be done. Assemble the released prisoners from the cellar. We will have to transport them back to La Trinidad with us. Ensure that we have ample stocks of food from the storeroom to feed all our people and have a work party report here to me. We are going to burn this nest of evil so that it will not be used as a haven for outlaws in the future. I don't know what the laws of Texas are regarding arson, but that is what I think should be done!'

Abbie paused in her report of the final hours of Hacienda Alvarez and stared silently into the flickering embers of the campfire. Captain David McHugh waited patiently for her to continue with her report. At length his temporary captain straightened herself, took a deep breath, and described how the body of Felipe, their only civilian casualty, had been buried with full military honours on a hillside facing Mexico and that one of the ex-prisoners had carved a simple headstone to mark the place.

The body of Antonio Alvarez and those of his men, together with the dead Comanche, were stacked in the dining room of the hacienda. All the rooms were amply doused with oil from the well-stocked store rooms and barrels of gunpowder placed where their explosions would do the most damage. Then the Rangers, the ex-prisoners and the well-guarded surviving outlaws evacuated the site and retreated to a safe location as Abbie lit a torch and tossed it into the room of the dead.

Hurriedly she had mounted her bay and, putting the spur to his flanks, she made haste to put a fair distance between herself and the anticipated inferno.

The oil-saturated timbers caught immediately and

the fire spread rapidly, followed by a series of loud booms as one after another the barrels detonated. The flames became a raging inferno as though Hell itself was trying to arise from the desert. The roof caved in, followed by the partial collapse of the outer and inner walls, and as the conflagration consumed the hacienda, Abbie had realized that her Texan mission was coming to an end.

Captain McHugh, though expressing his condolences over the death of Felipe, was lavish in his praise at the way in which Abbie had conducted what went down in Ranger history as the Alvarez operation. In return, he was able to provide solutions to a couple of minor mysteries that had remained unanswered. It will be remembered that as the Rangers had first entered La Trinidad they had seen the corpse of Benito Gomez, the late *El Caudillo*, hanging from the livery barn hoist. One of Padre Pedro's flock had finally let slip what had actually happened.

When Gomez had entered the town he had headed for a cantina to slake his thirst and had immediately been confronted by a group of fellow Mexicans who had suffered at the hands of him and his gang. As they were arguing what to do with him, he had suddenly collapsed and was already dead when he was hoisted and left swinging at the livery stable. The men responsible for stringing him up thought that their act might cause some of the more lawless elements of the town to see the error of their ways.

The similar hanging of Ace Lonergan was believed to have been done at the command of Antonio

Alvarez, who apparently had come to the conclusion that the former was drawing too much attention to himself and had failed to carry out his instructions to get rid of the Ranger presence.

The perpetrators had slipped into town and since they were his fellow gang members he had been easily persuaded to go with them unwittingly to the place of his own execution.

Abbie's work in La Trinidad was ended and she and the surviving members of her Colorado City posse were now eager to head north after a brief ceremony, during which they were officially discharged from the Ranger service. As she stood by her bay preparing to swing into the saddle to lead her group homeward, Captain McHugh came up to bid her goodbye. 'Goodbye, David,' Abbie said with a catch in her voice, 'Go home to that wife of yours on the Brazos! I would be happy if you had a twin brother around somewhere.'

McHugh reached forward to shake her hand and suddenly changed his mind and grabbed her in a fierce hug. 'Abbie, you're a true comrade and the best pal I've ever had. Take care of yourself and, rest assured, Texas will never forget the Pinfire Lady!'